"Well?" She Prodded.

He gripped her shoulders, resisting the urge to shake her. "Stop. Interrupting. Me."

Her chin bumped up and she glared at him through stormy eyes.

Suddenly he couldn't remember what it was he'd been about to say. All he could think was that this was what he'd wanted for the past two months. He wanted to sleep with her. To strip her clothes off, lay her bare before him in a proper bed and spend hours worshipping her body.

"Well?" she demanded again. "Is that the best you can do?"

"No," he said. "This is."

Cupping her jaw in his hands, he shut her up the best way he knew how. He kissed her.

Dear Reader,

Affair with the Rebel Heiress is a very special book for me, not only because I love these characters and felt honored to tell their story (I always feel that way), but also because it marks an anniversary for me: it's my tenth book!

I've been reading romances since I was eleven. I literally grew up reading Harlequin Romance and Presents novels, Silhouette Desire books and the old Bantam Loveswept titles. I spent so much money at the bookstore that my parents actually complained about it. (How crazy is that?)

Every time I turn in a book, or see the cover for the first time, or hold my book in my hands, I get this electric shock of excitement. I love being part of the Harlequin family, and I can't tell you how proud I am to have my tenth book with them out this month!

Now, about that book... Some of you may remember Kitty Biedermann from *Baby Benefits,* which was out in October 2008. She was Derek Messina's fiancée. She was the classic romance novel "other woman"— manipulative and self-centered. When I decided I wanted her to be the heroine of my next book, I knew I was facing a challenge. How could I transform her into a character people would love? I gave her plenty of spunk and sass along with a secret she'll go to great lengths to keep hidden. And of course, she had to have a great hero with whom to match wits. Enter Ford Langley, a charming business tycoon who's just not the type to back down from a challenge.

Did I pull it off? I think so. I hope you do, too!

Emily McKay

EMILY McKAY

AFFAIR WITH THE REBEL HEIRESS

Silhouette® Desire

Published by Silhouette Books

America's Publisher of Contemporary Romance

SILHOUETTE BOOKS

ISBN-13: 978-0-373-73003-2

Recycling programs
for this product may
not exist in your area.

AFFAIR WITH THE REBEL HEIRESS

Printed in U.S.A.

Books by Emily McKay

Silhouette Desire

Surrogate and Wife #1710
Baby on the Billionaire's Doorstep #1866
Baby Benefits #1902
Tempted Into the Tycoon's Trap #1922
In the Tycoon's Debt #1967
Affair with the Rebel Heiress #1990

EMILY McKAY

has been reading romance novels since she was eleven years old. Her first Harlequin Romance came free in a box of Hefty garbage bags. She has been reading and loving romance novels ever since. She lives in Texas with her husband, her newborn daughter and too many pets. Her books have been finalists for RWA's Golden Heart Award, the Write Touch Readers' Award and the Gayle Wilson Award of Excellence. Her debut novel, *Baby, Be Mine,* was a RITA® Award finalist for Best First Book and Best Short Contemporary. To learn more, visit her Web site at www.EmilyMcKay.com.

For my mother, Judy Beierle, who has taught me
over and over to smile in the face of adversity,
to meet challenges with bravery and hope, and to always,
always find something to laugh about.

One

Kitty Biedermann hated Texas.

That single thought had echoed through her mind from the time the flight attendant had said the words "unscheduled landing in Midland, Texas," until this moment, five hours later, when she found herself sitting in the bar adjacent the seedy motel in which she would be forced to spend the night.

The last time she'd been in Texas, she'd been dumped by her fiancé. Of course, he hadn't been just any old fiancé. He'd been the man she'd handpicked to save Biedermann Jewelry from financial ruin. So being dumped hadn't resulted in mere public humiliation or simple heartbreak. It meant the end of Biedermann Jewelry. So it was understandable that Kitty held a bit of grudge, not just against Derek Messina, but against the whole damn state.

Since being dumped by Derek, her situation had gone from bad to worse to desperate. She had needed Derek.

From the time she was a child, she'd been raised with one purpose—to land a husband with the smarts and business savvy to run Biedermann's. When Derek hadn't wanted her, she'd remained undaunted. But now, after six months of working her way through every single, eligible straight man she knew, she was beginning to feel...well, daunted.

With this latest trip to Palm Beach, she'd been scraping the bottom of the barrel. Geoffrey barely had two functioning synapses to rub together, but at least he could read, write and looked damn good in a suit. But even as meager as his qualifications had been, he hadn't wanted her.

Biedermann's meant everything to her. It was slipping through her fingers and there didn't seem to be anything she could do to catch it.

Now, with her elbows propped on the suspiciously sticky bar top and her chin propped in her palms, she stared at the murky green depths of her salt-rimmed margarita glass. She gave the glass a little shake, watching as the ice cubes within tumbled to the bottom of the glass. A lifetime of planning had fallen apart just as quickly. Was this rock bottom?

Her throat tightened against despair. Immediately she straightened, blinking in surprise. She was not given to fits of self-pity. Certainly not in public.

She shook her glass again, studying the contents. Exactly what was in this margarita? After a mere two drinks she should not be succumbing to such maudlin emotions.

Maybe this was what she got for giving the bartender a hard time. When she'd ordered a Pinot Grigio, he'd asked, "Is that like a wine cooler?" Apparently she shouldn't have doubted him when he said he'd make her a drink strong enough to knock her on her pampered, scrawny butt.

She was still contemplating the contents of her drink when she happened to glance toward the door and saw *him* striding in.

It was as if someone tossed a bucket of icy water on her. Every cell in her body snapped to life in pure visceral response. The stranger was tall and lean, somehow managing to look lanky but well-built all at the same time. He was dressed simply in well-worn jeans and a T-shirt that stretched taut across his shoulders, but hung loose over his abdomen. No beer belly on this guy. A cowboy hat sat cockeyed on his head, but he wore scuffed work boots instead of the cowboy boots she expected.

Her first thought—when she was capable of thought again—was, *Now* this *is a cowboy. This* was what women the world over romanticized. *This* was a man at his most basic. Most masculine.

Even from across the room, her body responded to him instantly, pumping endorphins down to the tips of her curling toes. Funny, because she'd always preferred her men sophisticated and suave. As well-groomed as they were well-educated.

She was, in fact, so distracted by this mystery cowboy who'd just sauntered in that she didn't see the other guy sidling up to her. The rough hand on her arm was her first clue someone had claimed the stool beside hers. Swiveling around, she realized that hand belonged to a guy who could not have been more different than the cowboy who'd snagged her attention. This man was short and, um…plump. He was bald except for a few wisps of hair grown long, combed over and plastered down with what she could only hope was some sort of styling product. His cheeks were rosy, his nose bulbous. He looked vaguely familiar, though she couldn't possibly have met him before.

"Well, hello there, little lady." He stroked a hand up her arm. "Whadda say we getcha some'tem cold to drink and we scoot on out to that there dance floor?"

"Pardon?" She—barely—suppressed a shiver of disgust at his touch. She tried to wiggle free from his grasp, but he had boxed her in between the bar and the woman on the stool beside her.

Why was he rubbing her arm like that? Did she know this man? After all, he *did* look familiar.

"You wanna take a turn around the room?"

"A turn at what?" she asked, genuinely not understanding him. She spoke four languages, for goodness' sake, but Texan was not one of them.

The man frowned. "Are you makin' fun a me?"

"No," she protested. Unfortunately, it was then that

she figured out where she knew him from. "Elmer Fudd!" she blurted out. "You look like Elmer Fudd!"

Normally, she would not have said anything, but she'd already gulped down two of those wicked margaritas. And all she'd eaten since lunch was a packet of airline peanuts. So her tongue was looser than normal.

Indignation settled over his pudgy features. He leaned toward her, scowling. "Whadja call me?"

"I…I didn't mean it as an insult."

"You *are* makin' fun a me." The man's face flushed red, only increasing his resemblance to the cartoon hunter.

"No! I…I…I…"

And there it was. She, who almost always knew exactly what to say and who could talk herself into and out of almost any situation, for better or for worse, was speechless. Horribly so.

She'd unintentionally insulted and offended a man who was probably armed right now. This was it. She was going to die. Alone. Miserable. In Texas. Murdered in a fit of rage. By a man who looked like Elmer Fudd.

Ford Langley could see trouble coming the second he stepped into The Dry Well, his favorite bar in Midland.

The Well was the kind of seedy dive that rednecks and oil rig workers had been coming to, through boom and bust, for sixty years or so. Since the Green Energy branch of FMJ, Ford's company, leased land for their wind turbines from a lot of the people in here, he figured they all knew who he was and how much he was worth. They just didn't care. Frankly, it was a relief places like this still existed in the world.

It was not, however, the kind of place women wore couture suits and designer shoes. Ford had three sisters with expensive taste. He knew a five-hundred-dollar pair of shoes when he saw them.

The woman sitting at the bar looked startlingly out of place. He'd never seen her there before. He came to The Well almost every time he visited Midland, and he definitely would have remembered this broad.

The word *broad* filtered through and stuck in his mind, because that's exactly what she looked like. The sexy broad who ambles into the PI's office in an old film noir movie. Lustrous flowing hair, long silk-clad legs, bright red lipstick, gut-wrenching sex appeal. With just enough wide-eyed innocence thrown in to make a man want to be the one to save her. Even though he knew instinctively that he would get kicked in the teeth for his trouble.

To make matters worse, she was talking to Dale Martin, who, Ford knew, had been going through a rough divorce. Dale had undoubtedly come in looking for what The Well provided best: booze, brawls and one-night stands. Given how completely out of his league the woman was, Ford could already guess which Dale was going to get.

When Ford heard Dale's distinctive drawl rising above the blare of the jukebox, Ford moved through the crowd, closing in on the brewing conflict, hoping he could cut trouble off at the pass.

He approached just in time to hear Dale accuse her of making fun of him. Hiding his cringe, Ford slung an arm around the woman's shoulders.

The stubborn woman tried to pull out of his grasp, but he held her firm. "I will—"

"Dale, buddy," he continued before she could ruin his efforts. "I see you met my date." He sent the woman a pointed look, hoping she'd take the hint and stop trying to squirm away. "Sugar, did you introduce yourself to my buddy, Dale?"

"It's Kitty," she snapped.

Dale was looking from him to her with a baffled expression. Which was fine, because Ford figured confused was better than furious.

"Right, sugar." Ford gave her shoulder an obvious squeeze. Winking at Dale, he added, "Kitty here's one of those feminist types."

She blinked, as if having trouble keeping up with the conversation. "Insisting that I be called by my given name and not some generic endearment does not make me—"

"She's a bit prickly, too." Based on her accent, he made a guess. "You know how Yankees are, Dale."

"I am not prickly," she protested.

But with Ford's last comment, a smile spread across Dale's face and at her protest, he burst out laughing, having forgotten or excused whatever she'd said to offend him. After all, she was a Yankee and obviously couldn't be expected to know better.

With Dale sufficiently distracted, Ford tugged the

delectable Kitty off her stool and nudged her toward The Well's crowded dance floor. "Come on. Why don't you show me what you can do in those fancy shoes of yours, sugar?"

At "sugar" he gave Dale another exaggerated wink. She, of course, squeaked an indignant protest, which only made Dale laugh harder.

When they were out of Dale's hearing range, she once again tried to pull away from him. "Thank you, I'm sure. But I could have handled him myself. So you can't seriously expect me to dance with you."

"'Course I do. Dale's watching."

Before she could voice any more protests, or worse, undermine all his hard work, he stepped onto the dance floor, spun her to face him and pulled her close. The second he felt her body pressed to his, he had to ask himself, had he really orchestrated all of that to avoid a fight or had he been angling for this all along?

She was taller than she'd looked sitting on the stool. With her heels on, her head came up past his chin, which was rare, since he dwarfed most women. As he'd suspected, her boxy suit hid a figure that was nicely rounded without being plump. She was delectably, voluptuously curved.

He felt the sharp bite of lust deep in his gut. Maybe he shouldn't have been surprised. He lived a fairly high-profile life back in San Francisco. As a result, he picked his lovers carefully for their discretion, sophistication and lack of expectations. He had enough responsibility without saddling himself with a spouse.

Unfortunately, it had been nearly six months since his previous girlfriend, Rochelle, had gone out for lunch one day with a friend who had kids and came home dreaming of designer diaper bags. He'd been happy to dodge that bullet and hadn't been in a hurry to find someone to replace her. Which probably explained his strong reaction to this woman. Kitty, she'd said her name was.

As he moved her into a shuffle of a Texas two-step, he felt her body relax against his. If his instincts were right, Kitty was smart, beautiful and used to taking care of herself. In short, she was exactly his sort of woman. She just may be the most interesting thing that had happened to him in a long time.

Kitty had never before found herself in this situation. Naturally she often danced with men she'd only just met. But she kept very careful tabs on the social scene in Manhattan. As a result, she usually knew the net worth, family history and sexual inclinations of every male in the room.

What some might consider mere gossip, she considered her professional obligation. She was in no position to date, marry or even notice a man who couldn't bring his own personal fortune to her family coffers. Unfortunately, ever since Suzy Snark had caught Kitty in her sights, the business of finding a rich husband had become increasingly difficult. Derek—damn him—had been the perfect choice. Until he'd gone and fallen in love.

But the truth was, she was tired of planning every move she made. This stranger with whom she was dancing, this cowboy, this man she'd never see again after tonight, made her pulse quicken.

From the moment she'd seen him sauntering through the door to the instant he'd pulled her body against his, she'd felt more alive than she had in months. Years, maybe. Somehow the scent of him, masculine and spicy, rose up from his chest and cut through the stench of stale smoke and cheap beer. His shoulders and arms were firm and muscular without being bulky. He had the physique of a man who worked for a living. Who lifted heavy things and shouldered massive burdens. The hand that cradled hers was slightly rough. This was a man who'd never had a manicure, never taken a Pilates class and probably didn't own a suit.

In short, he was a real man. Unlike the pampered men of her acquaintance. Most of whom, she was sorry to say, were likable, but were just a little bit…well, that is to say…well, they were sissies. And until this moment, she'd never realized that bothered her. She'd never known she wanted anything else.

Her face was only inches from his shirt and she had to fight against the sudden impulse to bury her nose in his chest. To rub her cheek against his sternum like a cat marking her territory.

It had been so long since she felt this kind of instant sexual attraction to someone. Geesh, had she ever felt this kind of attraction? She didn't think so.

Not that she planned on acting on it. A one-night stand was *so* not part of her five-year plan.

"I don't even know your name," she muttered aloud.

"Ford," he murmured.

He'd ducked his head before speaking so the word came out as warmth brushing past her ear. She suppressed a shiver.

"Like the car?" she asked.

He chuckled. "Yep. Like the car."

Geesh, indeed. Even his name was masculine. Why couldn't he have had a name that was just a bit more androgynous? Like Gene or Pat. Or BMW.

She didn't manage to stifle her chuckle.

"You're imagining me named after other car brands, aren't you?"

Her gaze shot to his. "How did you know?"

"It's pretty common. People usually think one of two things and you just seemed the type to wonder, 'What if he'd been named Chevy?'"

"Are you saying I'm predictable?" Even though the lighting was dim, she could see that his eyes were whiskey-brown. And just as intoxicating as the tequila in her drink.

"Not at all," he reassured her. "You could have been thinking Dodge."

"It was BMW, actually. I can't see you as something as clunky as a Dodge." Was she *flirting* with him? What was wrong with her?

"So you're a woman who appreciates precision engineering."

Actually, I'm a woman who enjoys precision in everything.

The words had been on the tip of her tongue. Thank God she swallowed them. Instead she asked, "What's the second?"

"Second what?"

"You said people usually think one of two things. If the first is other car names, then what's the second?"

His lips quirked in either amusement or chagrin. "They wonder if I was conceived in the back of a Ford."

"Ah." Perhaps that had been chagrin, then. And was that the faintest hint of pink creeping into his cheeks? As if he were just a tad embarrassed. "And were you?"

"That," he said firmly, "is a question I was never brave enough to ask my parents." They both chuckled then. A moment later he added, "But I have three sisters and their names are not Mattress, Kitchen Table and Sofa, so I think I'm safe."

She nearly asked what the names of his three sisters were, but she stopped herself. Somehow that seemed inappropriate. More personal, even, than the discussion of his conception. She didn't know Ford. Didn't want to know him longer than the length of this song. Personal details like the names of his sisters didn't matter. So instead, she gave in to her temptation to rest her cheek against the strong wall of his chest and to breathe in deeply.

After a moment he said, "I hope you don't judge Dale too harshly."

"Dale?"

"The guy hitting on you earlier."

"Ah. Him." She'd forgotten he even existed.

"He's been going through a rough divorce. His wife left him for a guy who's twenty-three years old."

"Ouch. That's got to be hard on the ego."

"Exactly. Which is why he's been a mite irritable lately. But what exactly did you say to him that made him so mad?"

She cringed, hesitating before answering him. "I said he looked like Elmer Fudd."

Ford seemed to be suppressing laughter. "I can't imagine why that offended him. Everybody loves Elmer Fudd."

"That's what I tried to tell him!"

They both chuckled. But then she looked up. For a moment, space seemed to telescope around them, blocking out everything else. The smoke, the crowd, even the blare of the music faded until all she could hear was the steady *thump-thump* of the bass echoing the thud of her heartbeat.

She felt her nerves prickle in anticipation. Desire, hot and heavy, unspooled through her body. Her very skin felt weighed down. Her thighs flushed with warmth.

Who knew that laughter could be such a turn-on?

Their feet stopped shuffling across the floor. That ridiculous grin seemed frozen on her face for an instant, but then it faded, melted away by the intensity of his gaze. There was a spot just over his ear where his otherwise straight hair curled. Before she could think, her fingers had moved to his temple to tease that wayward lock of hair.

He took her hand in his, stilling her fingers. He cleared his throat, and she expected him to say something, something funny maybe, something to lighten the tension between them, but he said nothing.

Who had ever imagined that she'd feel this needy lust for a stranger? Not just a stranger, but a cowboy. A Texan. When she'd sworn she'd never even set foot in this damn state again. She *so* hadn't seen this coming.

That's when it hit her. Here, tonight, was a night out of time. She would never be here again. She would never see him again.

In this strange place, with this man she didn't know, she had complete immunity. Freedom from her well-planned life. From her routines and her expectations of herself.

Tonight she could do whatever she wanted with no consequences. She could allow herself to do what she would normally *never* do. She could be stupid and reckless.

Without giving herself the chance to harbor second thoughts, she rose up on her toes and pressed her lips to his. His mouth moved over hers with a heated intensity. The sensual promise in his kiss made her shiver. She arched against him, letting her body answer the call of his. She slipped her hand into his and walked off the dance floor, tugging him along behind her.

As she wove her way through the crowd, the tempo of her blood picked up. After a lifetime of carefully planning, of controlling her actions and emotions, he could be her one rebellion. Tonight could be a vacation from her life.

And even if this was a mistake, he'd make sure she didn't regret it.

Two

Two months later

"You've got to stop moping around," Jonathon Bagdon said, then added, "And get your feet off my desk."

Ford, who'd been sitting with his work boots propped up on the edge of Jonathon's desk while he scraped the tip of his pocketknife under his nails, looked up for the first time since his business partner walked in the room. "What?"

Jonathon swatted at Ford's boots with the leather-clad portfolio he'd been carrying. "Keep your feet off my desk. Christ, it's like you're ten."

Ford's feet, which had been crossed at the ankles,

slid off Jonathon's desk. He lowered them to the floor and ignored the insult.

"The desk is worth twenty thousand dollars. Try not to scuff it."

Finally Ford looked up at his friend, taking in the scowl. He glanced over at Matt, the third partner in their odd little triumvirate, who sat on the sofa, with one leg propped on the opposite knee and a laptop poised on the knee. "Who shoved a stick up his ass this morning?" Ford asked Matt.

Matt continued typing frenetically while he said, "Ignore him. He's just trying to bait you. He doesn't give a damn about the desk."

Ford looked from one to the other, suddenly feeling slightly off-kilter. Together the three of them formed FMJ, Inc. He'd known these men since they were kids. They'd first gone into business together when they were twelve and Jonathon had talked them into pooling their money to run the snack shack at the community rec center for the summer. One financially lucrative endeavor had led to another until here they were, twenty years later, the CEO, CFO and CTO of FMJ, a company which they'd founded while still in college and which had made them all disgustingly rich.

Jonathon, though always impeccably dressed and by far the most organized of the three, might impress some as overly persnickety. But those were only the people who didn't know him, the people who were bound to underestimate him. It was a mistake few people made more than once.

In reality, it was unlike Jonathon to care whether or not his desk was scuffed, regardless of how much it was worth.

Still, to mollify Jonathon, Ford abandoned the chair he'd been sitting in and returned to his own desk. Since they worked so closely together, they didn't have individual offices. Instead, they'd converted the entire top floor of FMJ's Palo Alto headquarters to a shared office. On one end sat Jonathon's twenty-thousand-dollar art deco monstrosity. The other end was lined with three worktables, every inch of them covered by computers and gadgets in various stages of dissection. In the middle sat Ford's desk, a sleek modern job the building's interior designer had picked out for him.

With a shrug, he asked, "Is Matt right? You just trying to get a rise out of me?"

Jonathon flashed him a cocky grin. "Well, you're talking now, aren't you?"

"I wasn't before?"

"No. You've been picking at your nails for an hour now. You haven't heard a word I've said."

"Not true," Ford protested. "You've been babbling about how you think it's time we diversify again. You've rambled on and on about half a dozen companies that are about to be delisted by the NYSE, but that you think could be retooled to be profitable again. You and Matt voted while I was in China visiting the new plant and you've already started to put together the offer. Have I left anything out?"

"And…" Jonathon prodded.

"And what?" Ford asked. When Jonathon gave an exasperated sigh and plopped back in his chair, Ford shot a questioning look at Matt, who was still typing away. "And what?"

Matt, who'd always had the uncanny ability to hold a conversation while solving some engineering problem, gave a few more clicks before shutting his laptop. "He's waiting for you to voice an opinion. You're the CEO. You get final vote."

FMJ specialized in taking over flailing businesses and turning them around, much like the snack shack they'd whipped into prosperity all those years ago. Jonathon used his wizardry to streamline the company's finances. Matt, with his engineering background, inevitably developed innovations that helped turn the company around. Ford's own role in their magic act was a little more vague.

Ford had a way with people. Inevitably, when FMJ took over a company, there was resentment from the ownership and employees. People resisted, even feared, change. And that's where Ford came in. He talked to them. Smoothed the way. Convinced them that FMJ was a company they could trust.

He flashed a smile at Matt. "I can do my part no matter what the company is. Why do I need to vote?"

While he spoke, he absently opened his desk drawer and tossed the pocketknife in. As if of their own accord, his fingers drifted to the delicate gold earring he kept stored in the right-hand corner.

The earring was shaped like a bird, some kind of sea

bird, if he wasn't mistaken. Its wings were outstretched as if it were diving for a fish, its motion and yearning captured in perfect miniscule detail.

Ford's fingertip barely grazed the length of its wingspan before he jerked his hand out and slammed the drawer shut.

It was her earring. Kitty Biedermann's. The woman from the bar in Texas.

He'd discovered it in the front of his rented pickup when he'd gone to turn the truck in. Now he wished he'd left it there. It wasn't like he was going to actually return the earring to its owner.

Yes, when he'd first found the earring, he'd had Wendy, FMJ's executive assistant, look Kitty up, just to see how hard it would be to hunt her down. But then Kitty Biedermann turned out to be a jewelry store heiress.

What was he going to do, fly to New York to return the earring? He was guessing she didn't want to see him again any more than he wanted to see her. But now he was stuck with this stupid bird earring.

As much to distract himself as anything, he rocked back in his chair and said, "Okay, let's buy a company. What do they do again?"

"What do you mean, what do they do?" Jonathon grumbled. "This is the company you researched."

Ford nudged his foot against the edge of the desk and set his chair to bobbing. "What are you taking about? I didn't research a company."

"Sure you did." Jonathon held out the portfolio.

When Ford didn't take it, Jonathon settled for tossing in on Ford's desk. "The same day I sent out that first list of companies to consider, you e-mailed Wendy and told her to dig up anything she could find on Biedermann Jewelry. Since you seemed interested in them, Matt and I voted and…"

Listening to his partner talk, Ford let his chair rock forward and his feet drop to the floor. With a growing sense of dread, he flipped open the portfolio. And there was the proposal. To buy Biedermann Jewelry.

His stomach clenched like he'd been sucker punched.

Had Wendy misunderstood his casual, *Hey, see what you can find out about Kitty Biedermann?* But of course Wendy had. She was obsessively thorough and eager to please.

With forced nonchalance he asked, "Have you put a lot of work into this deal yet?"

"A couple hundred man hours," Jonathon hedged. "Biedermann's is circling the drain. We need to move fast."

Matt normally wasn't the most intuitive guy. But he must have heard something in Ford's voice, because he asked, "What's up, Ford? You having doubts?"

"It's a pretty risky deal," he said simply. Maybe he could gently redirect their attention.

But Jonathon shook his head. "It isn't really. Biedermann's has always been a strong company. They've been undervalued ever since Isaac Biedermann died last year. But I can turn them around." Jonathon's lips quirked in one of his rare grins. "Kind of looking forward to the challenge, actually."

Ford had seen that look in Jonathon's eyes before. Jonathon was ready to gobble up Biedermann's. Any minute now he'd be picking his teeth with the bones of Biedermann's carcass.

Unless Ford stopped him.

Which he could do. All he'd have to do is explain about Kitty. And the earring.

But what was he really supposed to say? *Don't buy the company because I slept with her?* He usually preferred relationships to last a little longer than one night, but he wasn't above the occasional fling when the chance presented itself. He'd never had a problem walking away the next day. He just wasn't a long-term kind of guy. He wouldn't even remember her name if it hadn't been for that lost earring.

"So what do you say?" Jonathon asked. "We all in?"

"Sure." And he sounded convincingly casual about it, too. He pushed his chair back and stood. "Hey, I'm going to the gym. That damn chair makes my back hurt."

"Don't be gone long. We've got work to do."

"When do you leave for New York?" he asked.

"Not me, we," Jonathon corrected. "As soon as I can get the board to agree to a meeting."

"Great." It looked like he was going to be able to return that earring after all.

Kitty sat at the head of the conference table, concentrating all of her considerable acting skill on looking relaxed. Today was the first of what would probably be many meetings to negotiate the deal with FMJ. She would never feel good about this, but what choice did she have? Everything she'd tried on her own had blown up in her face. Marty, Biedermann's CFO, had assured her this was her only option. Her last, best hope to salvage anything from Biedermann's.

Still, the thought of selling the company twisted her gut into achy knots. Beidermann's had been in her family since her great-great-grandfather had moved to New York from Germany and opened the first store in 1868. For her, Biedermann's wasn't just a company, it was her history, her heritage. Her family.

But it was also her responsibility. And if she couldn't save it herself, then she'd hand it over to someone who could, even if doing so made her stomach feel like it was about to flip itself inside out.

She should be more comfortable sitting at this table than most people were in their own bedrooms. And yet she found herself strumming her fingers against the gleaming wood as she fought nausea.

Beside her, Marty rested his hand over hers. He seemed to be aiming for reassuring, but his touch sent a shiver of disgust through her.

He stroked the backs of her fingers. "Everything will be all right."

She stiffened, jerking her hand out from under his. "I beg your pardon?"

"You seemed nervous."

"Nonsense." Still, she buried her hand in her lap.

She didn't handle sympathy well under normal circumstances. Now it made her feel like she was going to shatter. He looked pointedly at the spot on the table she'd been drumming on, to which she replied, "I'm impatient. They're seven minutes late and I have a reservation for lunch at Bruno's."

Marty's lips twitched. "You don't have to pretend with me."

Something like panic clutched her heart. So, he thought he saw right through her. Well, others had thought that before. "Don't be ridiculous, Marty. I've been pretending to be interested in your conversations for years. I'm certainly not going to stop now."

For an instant, a stricken expression crossed his face and regret bit through her nerves. Dang it. Why did she say things like that? Why was it that whenever she was backed into a corner, she came out fighting?

She was still contemplating apologizing when the door opened and Casey stuck her head through. "Mr. Ford Langley and Mr. Jonathon Bagdon are here."

Awash in confusion, she nearly leaped to her feet. "Ford Langley? Is here?"

Then she felt Marty's steady hand on hers again. "Mr. Langley's the CEO of FMJ. He's come in person for the negotiations."

She stared blankly at Marty, her mind running circles around one thought. Ford Langley.

He was here? He was the CEO of FMJ? Impossible. Ford Langley was an ignorant cowboy. She'd left him in Texas and would never see him again.

She must have misheard. Or misunderstood her assistant just now. Or misremembered the name of the stranger she'd slept with. Or perhaps through some cruel trick of fate, the CEO of FMJ and the stranger shared the same odd name.

Each of these possibilities thundered through her mind as she struggled to regain her composure. Mistaking her confusion, Marty must have spoken for her and told Casey to show in the people from FMJ.

She barely had time to school her panic into a semblance of calm before the door to the conference room swung open and there he was. Fate had pulled a much crueler trick on her than merely giving two men the same name. No, fate had tricked her into selling her beloved company to the same man to whom she'd already given her body.

What had he expected?

Okay, he hadn't thought she'd jump up, run across the room and throw her arms around him. But he sure as hell hadn't expected the complete lack of response. The coolly dismissive blank stare. As if she didn't recognize him at all. As if he were beneath her notice.

Her gaze barely flickered over him as she looked from him to Jonathon. Then she glanced away, looking bored. Someone from Biedermann's had stood and was making introductions. Ford shook hands at the right moment, filing away the name and face of Kitty's CFO.

She looked good. Lovely, in fact. As smoothly polished as the one-dimensional woman in the Nagel painting poster he'd had on his wall as a teenager. Beautiful. Pale. Flat.

Gone was the vibrant woman he'd danced with in The Well two months ago. By the time the introductions were done, one thing had become clear. She was going to pretend they'd never met before. She was going to sit through this meeting all the while ignoring the fact that they'd once slept together. That he'd touched her bare skin, caressed her thighs, felt her body tremble with release.

Which was exactly what he should do, too. Hell, wasn't that what he had *planned* on doing?

Just as Jonathon was pulling out his chair, Ford said, "Before we get started, I wonder if I could have a word alone with Ms. Biedermann."

Jonathon sent him a raised-eyebrowed, do-you-know-what-you're-doing? kind of look. Kitty's CFO hovered by her side, like an overly protective Chihuahua.

Ford gave the man his most reassuring smile while nodding slightly at Jonathon. He knew Jonathon would back him up and get the other guy out of there. Jonathon wouldn't question his actions, even if Ford was doubting them himself.

Something was up with Kitty and he intended to find out what it was.

Kitty watched Marty leave the conference room, fighting the urge to scream. An image flashed through her mind of herself wild-eyed and disheveled, pulling at her hair and shouting "Deserter! Traitor!" like some mad Confederate general about to charge into battle and to his death, all alone after his men have seen reason and fled the field.

Clearly, she'd been watching too many old movies.

Obviously her time would have been better spent practicing her mental telepathy. Then she could have ordered Marty to stay. As it was, she couldn't protest without Ford realizing how much the prospect of being alone with him terrified her.

The moment the door shut, leaving them alone in the room, he crossed to her side. "Hello, Kitty."

She stood, nodding. Praying some response would spring to her lips. Something smart. Clever. Something that would cut him to the bone without seeming defensive.

Sadly nothing came to mind. So she left it at the nod.

"You look…" Then he hesitated, apparently unsure which adjective best described her.

"I believe 'well' is usually how one finishes that sentence." Oh, God. Why couldn't she just keep her mouth shut?

"That's not what I was going to say."

"Well, you seem to be having trouble finishing the sentence," she supplied. "Since I'm sure I look just fine and since I'd much rather get this over with than stand around exchanging pleasantries, I thought I'd move things along."

He raised his eyebrows as if taken aback by her tone. "You aren't curious why I'm here?"

That teasing tone stirred memories best left buried

in the recesses of her mind. Unfortunately, those pesky
memories rose up to swallow her whole, like a tsunami.

As if it were yesterday instead of two months or
more, she remembered what it had felt like to be held
in his arms. Cradled close to his body as they swayed
gently back and forth on the dance floor. The way he'd
smelled, musky yet clean against the sensory backdrop
of stale smoke and spilled beer. The way her body had
thrummed to life beneath his touch. The way she'd
quivered. The way she'd come.

She thrust aside the memories, praying he wouldn't
notice that her breath had quickened. Thankful he
couldn't hear the pounding of her heart or see the hardening of her nipples.

Hiding her discomfort behind a display of boredom,
she toyed with the papers on the table where she'd been
sitting. She couldn't stand to look at him, so she pretended to read through them as she said, "I know why
you're here. You came here to take control of Biedermann's." Thank God her voice didn't crack as she
spoke. It felt as if her heart did, but that at least she
could hide. For the first time since he walked into the
room, she met his gaze. "You can't honestly expect me
to welcome you. You're stealing the company I was
born to raise."

His expression hardened. "I'm not stealing anything.
FMJ is providing your failing company with some
much-needed cash. We're here to keep you in business."

"Oh, really. How generous of you." She buried all
her trepidation beneath a veneer of sarcasm. As she

always did. It was so much easier that way. "Since that's the case, why don't you just write out a nice hefty check and leave it on the table on your way out. I'll call you in a decade or so to let you know if it helped."

"A big, fat check might help if all you needed was an infusion of cash. But the truth is, Biedermann's needs a firm hand at the helm and you can't have one without the other. You know that's not how this works."

His words might have been easier to swallow if he'd sounded apologetic instead of annoyed. No, wait…there wasn't really any way that anything he said could be easier to swallow.

"No. Of course that's not how it works. You'll go over the company with a fine-toothed comb. You'll tear it apart, throw out the parts you don't like and hand the rest back in pieces. In the end, everything my family's worked for for five generations will be gone. All so you can turn a quick profit."

"Tell me something. Is that really what's bothering you?"

Of course it wasn't what was really bothering her. What was really bothering her was that he was here at all. Her safe, what-the-hell-I'm-stuck-in-Texas fling hadn't stayed where it was supposed to. In Texas. What was the point of having a fling with a stranger if the man ended up not being a stranger at all?

But she couldn't say that aloud. Especially given the way he was looking at her. With his expression so intense, so sexual, so completely unprofessional, it sent a wave of pure shock through her system.

"W-what do you mean?"

"Come on, Kitty. This anger you're clinging to isn't about Biedermann's at all. This is about what happened in Texas."

She quickly buried her shock beneath a veneer of disdain. "Texas. I'm surprised you'd have the guts to bring that up."

"You are?"

"Of course." She strolled to the other side of the conference table. "I'd think you would be the last person to want to hash that over. But since you brought it up, maybe you can answer a question for me. Was anything you told me true or was it all pretense?"

"What's that supposed to mean?"

"You know. That whole charade you put on to pick me up back in Texas. That aw-shucks, I'm just a simple cowboy trying to make a living act."

"I never said I was a cowboy."

"No. But you had to know that's what I thought."

"How exactly was I supposed to know that?" His facade of easy charm slipped for a moment and he plowed a hand through his hair in frustration. He sucked in a breath and pointed out in a slightly calmer tone, "You weren't exactly forthcoming about who you were, either."

"I did nothing wrong." True, she hadn't exactly presented him with her pedigree when they'd first met, but surely it didn't take a genius to see she didn't fit in at that bar. If there had been an obvious clue he didn't, either, she'd missed it entirely. She refused to let him paint himself the victim. "I don't have anything to apologize for. I'm not the one who pretended to be some down on his luck cowboy."

"No, you're just the one who gave me a fake phone number instead of admitting you didn't want to see me again."

"If you knew I didn't want to see you again," she asked, "then why did you go to the trouble of hunting me down?"

"I didn't hunt you down. What happened in Texas has nothing to do with FMJ's offer."

"Then how exactly did the offer come about anyway?" she asked. "If you didn't go back to work and say, 'Wow, that Kitty Biedermann must be really dumb to have fallen for my tired old lines. I bet we could just swoop in and buy that company right from under her.'"

His gaze narrowed to a glare. "You know that's not how it happened."

"Really? How would I know that? What do I really know about you other than the fact that you're willing to misrepresent yourself to get a woman into bed with you?"

"I never lied to you. Not once. And despite the fact that you're acting like a brat, I won't start now."

"Maybe you didn't lie outright, but you certainly misled me. Of course, maybe that's the only way you can get a woman into bed."

Ford just smiled. "You don't believe that. The sex

was great." He closed in on her, getting right in her face as if daring her to disagree.

God, she wanted to. That would serve him right.

But when she opened her mouth, she found the denial trapped inside her. Between the intensity of his eyes and the memories suddenly flooding her, she just couldn't muster up the lie.

Instead she said the only thing that popped into her mind. "You can't convince me that FMJ is prepared to buy Biedermann's solely so you can get laid."

He grinned wolfishly. "Boy, you think highly of yourself."

"You were the one who brought up sex," she pointed out.

"You didn't let me finish. I was going to close with the suggestion that we both try to forget it happened."

"Oh, I won't have any trouble with that," she lied easily, barely even cringing as she waited for the bolt of lightning to strike her down.

"Excellent." He bit off the word. "Then you agree from here on out, it's all business?"

"Absolutely." Her smiled felt so tight across her face she was surprised she could still breathe. But she kept it in place as she crossed back to the door.

Jonathon and Marty were waiting in the office outside the conference room. If they'd picked up on the tension, neither commented. Thank goodness. She simply wouldn't have had the strength to come up with any more lies today. Between the lies she'd told Ford and the lies she was telling herself, she was completely out.

"Everything okay?" Jonathon asked, more to Ford than to her.

However, she didn't give the treacherous bastard a chance to answer. Instead, she dug deep and pulled out one more lie. "Mr. Langley was just assuring me Biedermann's is going to be in great hands with you." She held out her hand to gesture him back into the conference room. "Why don't you come in and we'll talk money."

Kitty's head was pounding by the time she finally made it back to her office alone. The simple truth was nothing could have prepared her for this.

She thought she'd been ready, but she hadn't, really. Not to sit in a conference room and listen politely while strangers discussed her beloved Biedermann's— while they calmly talked about compensation packages. While they talked about key positions in the company they'd need to replace.

Oh, they'd started by reassuring her that she would stay on as president of the subsidiary, but she knew she wouldn't have control. Not really. She'd be a figurehead, at best. A pretty adornment to make things look good. It'd be pathetic if it wasn't so sad. But the really pathetic thing was she would let herself be used that way.

She loved Biedermann's. She'd do whatever it took to save it. Even if she had to sell her soul to the devil. Or in this case, Ford Langley.

Three

If she thought her day couldn't get any worse, she was wrong. She ran into Ford in the elevator bay.

"Fantastic," she muttered as she punched the elevator button. "Thousands of people work in this building and I get to ride down with you."

"I waited for you."

"How kind." She didn't bother to meet his gaze or to inject any real graciousness in her voice. She certainly hoped he wasn't so dense that he couldn't hear her sarcasm.

"I wanted to apologize." He seemed to be speaking through gritted teeth.

Well, she certainly wasn't going to make this any easier for him. "For your behavior earlier?" she asked as the elevator doors began to open. She prayed there'd be someone else in the car with them, but her prayers went unanswered. Which was the norm of late. "Don't worry. I didn't expect better behavior from you. After all, I know what Californians are like."

It was a twist of something he'd said to her at that bar in Texas, when he'd teased her about being a Yankee. His gaze flickered to hers and for a second they seemed to both be remembering that night.

Damn it, why had she brought that up? She didn't want to remind him about that. She certainly didn't want him to think she remembered that night with anything approaching word for word accuracy.

"What I meant," he said, following her into the elevator, "was that the meeting seemed hard for you. I can't imagine it's easy to sell a company that's been in your family for generations."

She shot him a scathing look. "Please don't tax your mental capacity trying to imagine it."

The doors closed, sealing them inside. For a moment he thought she'd say nothing more, just ride with him in silence. Maybe this was it. Maybe she really was as cool a number as she'd seemed in the boardroom. Maybe selling her family company meant nothing more to her than—

Then abruptly she let loose a bitter laugh.

Okay, maybe not.

"You want to know the really funny thing?" she asked as she punched the 1 button. "This is exactly what I was raised to do."

"Run Biedermann's?" he asked.

"Oh, God, no. Don't get me wrong. My father adored me. Treated me like an absolute princess. But he never thought I was capable of running Biedermann's. I was supposed to transform myself into the perfect wife. I was supposed to catch myself a rich husband to run Biedermann's for me."

She slanted him a look as if to assess his reaction. Her tongue darted out to slip along her lower lip and his body tightened in response. He was not supposed to want her. This was about business. Not sex. Now, if only his body would get that memo.

Apparently she'd gotten it though, because she continued on as if the energy between them wasn't charged with the memory of soul-scalding sex.

She shook her head wryly. "His attitude was archaic, but there you have it."

"So you decided to prove him wrong," he surmised.

"No, I didn't even do that. I really tried to marry the perfect man to take over Biedermann's. I had him all picked out. Even got him to propose." When the elevator doors didn't shut fast enough for her liking she started punching the close button repeatedly. "He just decided to marry someone else instead. I won't bore you with the details of my love life. Not when they're available online in several different gossip columns."

The elevator started to drop and again she laughed.

"See, that's the funny part, right? Flash-forward a year. I've made a complete mess running Biedermann's, just like my father predicted. You swoop in to rescue the company. FMJ is going to take care of everything. But—" she hastily added, as if he were about to argue with her. "I'll still get to play at being president of the company. You'll be watching over my shoulder, so there's no chance I'll make things worse. I'll just get to sit there, looking good, while a big strong man fixes things for me. It's the job I was raised to do."

"Kitty—" he began, but the doors opened and she cut him off as they did.

"My father would be so proud."

She said it with the cavalier indifference of someone who was truly in pain. But damn, she was good at hiding it.

If he hadn't met her under other circumstances, if he'd never seen her with her guard down, he'd probably even be fooled. But as it was, he saw right through her.

If she'd been weeping and moping, maybe he could have ignored her despair. Or handed her off into the care of someone who knew her better. But these bitter self-recriminations…well, he remembered how he'd felt after his father died. The grief, the anger, the guilt, all rolled into one. He wouldn't wish that on anyone.

He fell into step beside her, and said, "Look, you're going through a hard time. You shouldn't be alone tonight. It's Friday night. Why not let me take you out for—"

"It's not necessary. I have plans."

"Plans?" he asked. "After a day like today?"

She waved a hand, still putting on a brave face. "It's

something I couldn't get out of. A commitment from weeks ago."

He quirked an eyebrow, waiting for her to supply more information.

Finally she added, "It's a fundraiser for The Children's Medical Foundation. At The Pierre. Very posh. You wouldn't be comfortable there," she finished dismissively.

She was either trying to insult him or she'd made up the engagement to put him off. He didn't believe for a minute that she planned on going to this charity event, even if she had bought the tickets months ago. She was just trying to get rid of him. But he couldn't stand the thought of her all alone, wallowing in her misery.

"Great." Why not pretend to buy her story? "I'll come with you."

She shot him a look icy enough to freeze his eyebrows off.

Okay, so he couldn't exactly imagine Kitty wallowing in anything. Here in New York she was as cool and collected as they came.

But he'd seen her outside her element. He'd seen her vulnerable. He knew that a passionate, emotional woman lurked beneath the surface of her icy cool perfection. If he peeled back the layers to reveal that woman, he'd probably find someone who could use a shoulder to cry on.

Kitty stopped in the lobby, ignoring the other people filtering out onto the street. "You don't need to do that."

"I don't have plans."

"Your partner—"

"Has a teleconference with some people in China."

"Who called a meeting for a Saturday morning?" she pressed.

"You know what they say." He flashed a smile. "If you don't come in on Saturday, don't bother coming in on Sunday, either."

"I'm fine," she insisted.

But she wasn't. He could see the strain in the lines around her eyes and in the tightness of her mouth. Of course, there was a chance his attempt to be kind was only making matters worse, but his gut told him to keep pushing. He was almost past her defenses, but charm alone wouldn't get her to open up. He needed to change tactics.

"Oh, I get it," he said. "You don't want to be with me."

"Exactly."

"You're probably afraid of how you feel about me." A lock of her hair had fallen free of its twist. He reached out and gave it a quick tug before tucking it behind her ear. He let his fingers linger there, at the sensitive place along the back of her ear.

She rolled her eyes. "That's not going to work."

"What?" he asked innocently.

"You're trying to bait me," she accused.

"Hey, I understand. You don't want to be alone with me. Can't say I blame you." He dropped his eyes to her lips. He let himself remember what it had been like to kiss her. To feel her breath hot on his skin. When he met her gaze again, he knew she remembered it, too.

"It's probably wise. We should spend as little time together as possible."

Her breath seemed to catch in her throat and her tongue darted out to lick her bottom lip. Then she seemed to shake off the effects. Her eyes narrowed in obvious annoyance. "Fine." She turned and started to walk away. "If you're so desperate for something to do tonight that you'll pull that cheap trick, you can come along. But don't blame me if tickets to this fundraiser are outrageously expensive at the last minute."

He smiled as he fell into step beside her. The spark was back in her eyes. The bite was back in her words. She'd be fine.

"I'll pick you up at your place," he offered.

"That's not necessary."

"I don't mind."

"Well, I do," she countered. "You don't honestly think I'm going to tell you where I live, do you?"

"You don't honestly believe I don't already know, do you?"

She turned and shot him an assessing stare. "You know where I live? What did you do, hire a private investigator?"

"I didn't have to. Jonathon has a whole team that researches that kind of thing when we're looking to acquire a company."

"I don't know whether to be creeped out or impressed." She reached the street and raised her hand to hail a cab, but this time of night the streets were packed. "Creeped out wins, I think."

"This is just company policy."

"What, all's fair in love and war?" she asked with an edge to her voice.

"This isn't love or war. This is business."

He held her gaze as firmly as he said it.

She jerked her gaze away from his, turning her attention to the passing cabs on the street. "This may be only business to you. But for me, it's both love and war. I love Biedermann's. And I've spent the last six months fighting for its survival. This may not be personal for you, but it's deeply personal for me."

A look of surprise crossed her face. Like she hadn't meant to admit that. Or maybe she just wasn't used to talking about her emotions.

After a minute he said, "Maybe that's part of the problem."

"Part of what problem?" He was about to respond, but she stopped him before he could. "And don't you dare tell me that 'the problem' is that I care too much. That I'm too emotionally involved to make rational decisions. Because I don't believe that my emotional state has anything to do with the flagging economy or the fact that malls across America are doing lower volume sales across the board." Her voice rose as she spoke, betraying her frustration. "If I could miraculously turn off my emotions and stop caring about Biedermann's, it wouldn't make a bit of difference. So if it's all the same to you, I'm going to go right on caring passionately about—"

Her voice cracked and she started blinking rapidly. Like she was trying to hold back tears.

He reached out a hand to her. "Kitty, I'm sorry—"

But a cab finally pulled up before he could finish the sentence. "Don't be sorry," she ordered as she opened the door. "Just find a way to fix it. Because if you can't, then we're both screwed."

She didn't look back as she climbed into the cab. He watched her go in silence.

She was one tough cookie.

Every other woman he knew was more in touch with her emotions. Or—he corrected himself— maybe just more willing to use her emotions to get what she wanted. Any one of his sisters would have been boo-hooing up a storm halfway through the meeting. But Kitty had just sat there in silence. Listening to every word that was said, but commenting little herself.

If it hadn't been for her outburst in the elevator, he might never have known how upset she truly was. She was unlike any woman he'd ever known. She wasn't willing to use tears to get what she wanted. He had to admire that.

But in other ways, Kitty was exactly like the other women he knew. She herself had admitted that she'd been on the lookout for a rich husband.

But somehow the poor bastard had slipped away. Or the lucky bastard, as the case may be. Frankly, he didn't know whether to feel sorry for the guy or not. Kitty was a hell of a woman.

Sure, he'd used steak knives that were less sharp than her tongue, but for him, that was part of her charm. He had enough women in his life that he had to walk on eggshells around. Thank God he didn't want to get married. Otherwise he might be tempted to drop to his knees and propose right now. He nearly chuckled imagining the scathing response that would earn him.

Ford had developed a certain cynicism about the institution at a very young age. He'd been about nine or ten when he first discovered that his father had a long-term girlfriend living one town over. Eventually, that girlfriend had developed into a second family, complete with two curly-haired little girls, quite close in age to his own sister.

At first the way his father balanced both families disgusted Ford. By the time he reached adulthood himself, it was no longer his father's behavior that troubled him. By then he'd realized both his mother and the other woman knew about each other. They'd been content to let the situation slide. As long as there was enough money to go around.

Since his father's death, Patrice and Suz had become friends in some sick little way. As for the girls, they now treated each other like the sisters they were. He seemed to be the only one who found the situation odd.

Now, standing on the curb watching the spot where Kitty's taxi had disappeared into the night, Ford nearly laughed himself. If she thought her revelation about her family would scare him off, she had another think coming. His family had more drama than a Greek tragedy.

Ford tucked his hands into his pockets and started walking toward the nearest subway station. It wasn't far back to the hotel and it was a nice night. He might as well enjoy the weather.

Only then did he feel the earring still in his pocket. It was just as well he hadn't returned it to her today. She might have been tempted to cram it down his throat.

Kitty's apartment, a walk-up in the eclectic Murray Hill neighborhood, surprised him. He'd have pegged her for an Upper East Side girl, or at the very least he imagined her in some glossy new high-rise. Instead, she lived in a prewar building that had seen better years.

When she let him into her fourth-floor apartment she wasn't dressed yet. She left him waiting in her living room for nearly an hour. Probably just to tick him off.

Her apartment was smaller than he'd expected, sparsely furnished with a few antiques. With the exception of a couple of framed black-and-white family pictures, the walls were bare. Either her taste was minimalist or she hadn't lived here long.

Ford spent the time hanging out on the sofa, first answering his e-mail on his iPhone, then reviewing some specs Matt had sent him, and then finally playing Tetris on his phone.

He might have left, but the truth was, the tension was palpable. Too much remained unsaid between them.

Under any other circumstances, he would have let it slide, being something of an expert on unresolved emotional issues. But with Kitty, it was different. He'd never before been in a position where he'd have to work with a woman he'd slept with. The last thing he wanted was some emotional complication mucking up the coming negotiations. If she was going to have a problem working with him, he wanted to clear the air now.

Finally her bedroom door opened to reveal Kitty encased in a shimmering deep purple gown with a low-cut, heart-shaped neckline. Her dark hair fell in sleek waves about her shoulders. He nearly laughed at the expression of surprise that flickered across her face when she spied him.

He stood. "You look lovely."

She fell into step beside him, not bothering to suppress an exasperated sigh. "You're still here."

"Much to your disappointment, I'm sure." He put a hand at her back to guide her to the door, only to discover a generous expanse of naked skin.

"Not at all," she murmured, suddenly all charm. "I had trouble with my zipper. You can't imagine how worried I was you might get tired of waiting and leave."

"Trouble with your zipper? For over an hour?"

"It's a long zipper."

He leaned away to look pointedly at the back of her dress. A delicate triad of beaded straps criss-crossed at her shoulders. Her skin was left bare all the way to just below her waist. The sparkling fabric molded to her bottom before falling in a straight line to the floor.

Just over the crest of her bottom he could see the faint outline of the zipper hidden in the seam. It couldn't have been more than four inches long.

"So I see."

Kitty was no scrawny fashion model. She had a body that managed to be both slender and voluptuous. Her bottom was lusciously rounded. Just looking at it made his blood throb with lust.

She elbowed him in a way that was both playful and seductive. "Stop looking at my zipper," she murmured huskily as she locked her door.

He shrugged as they started down the stairs. "If you don't want people looking at your *zipper*, you shouldn't display it quite so prominently."

"That's sexist," she chided.

"No, it would be sexist if we were at work and I ordered you to display your zipper. Or I hired you or fired you based on the size of your zipper. But this is a social situation, so I don't think either of those apply. Besides, a woman doesn't wear a dress like that unless she wants to be looked at."

He hailed a cab when they reached the street.

Kitty frowned, her bottom lip jutting forward in a pout. "Oh. We're going in a cab. How…prosaic."

"I try to avoid hiring a driver when I come to the city. They spend too much time looking for parking and driving around. It's a waste of gas and resources." He held open the cab door for her, admiring the swath of leg revealed as she slid into the car.

"Hmm. Like I said. How prosaic."

He climbed in beside her. "Being aware of the environment isn't prosaic." A hint of his annoyance slipped into his tone. "FMJ has made most of its money in green industries. Our image as a green company is a priority. Not just for the company, but for all of us."

She yawned delicately, but with obvious boredom. Annoyed by her attitude, he nearly called her on it, but before he could, it hit him. "You're doing this on purpose, aren't you?"

She looked taken aback. "I...I don't know what you mean. Doing what?"

"This." He gestured toward her body-skimming dress. "The sexpot dress. The self-indulgent pout. The childish behavior. It's all a way of keeping me off balance."

She blinked, and he couldn't tell if he'd insulted her or if she was merely surprised he'd seen through her. "You're just trying to distract me. To avoid that conversation we need to have."

"However did you get that idea?"

"Probably because you've been pushing me away ever since I walked into the conference room today. You've made it obvious that you don't want to relinquish control of Biedermann's. You may have fooled everyone else into thinking that's the only thing going on. But I can see right through you. I know the truth."

Oh, God. What did he mean? He knew *the truth?* What truth? That she was a total fraud? That she had no idea what she was doing?

He leaned closer, a seductive grin on his face. "I know what you're really afraid of."

"Afraid of?" she squeaked.

He brushed his thumb across her lower lip, once again sparking the desire that heated her blood every time he touched her.

She should not be attracted to him. He was so not what she needed right now. Or ever, for that matter. Geesh, he wasn't even wearing a tux. Okay, so he looked fabulous in an Armani jacket thrown over a gray cashmere sweater and black pants. And, yes, the understated elegance of his outfit made him look outrageously masculine. Never mind that he carried it off. Never mind that the day's worth of stubble on his jaw made her fingertips tingle with the urge to touch him. Never mind that she could tell already all the other men at the fundraiser would look overdressed and foppish by comparison. She couldn't possibly be attracted to a man who didn't even know when to wear a tie.

"Yes," he continued. "You're afraid of the attraction between us."

As his words registered, she was flooded with an odd sense of relief. He was still talking about sex. About what had happened between them in Texas.

Maybe it shouldn't have made her feel better, but somehow it did. Physical intimacy she could handle. Men had been pursuing her since she hit puberty. She knew how to handle that. She knew how to entice without promising anything. To lure and manipulate a man while staying just out of his reach.

What she didn't know was how to handle a man who was interested in her. Not her body. Not her net worth, but her.

Thank God, Ford was proving no different than any other man she'd ever met. She'd learned long ago the secret to keeping men at arm's length.

The mere suggestion of sex was enough to distract the average man. The possibility that you might one day have sex with him made most men so befuddled they never bothered to look beneath the surface.

To that end, she let herself sway toward him slightly, as if she couldn't resist his draw. Then she ran her tongue over the spot on her lip that he'd touched. It was a gesture sure to entice him, but she found it disconcertingly intimate. She could almost taste him on her tongue.

Suddenly memories flooded her of their one night together. How could she have forgotten what it had been like to kiss him? To feel his hands on her body? To give herself over so completely to his touch?

She felt her breath catch in her chest, found herself leaning toward him, not in a calculated way, but as if he were a magnet and the heart pounding away in her chest were made of iron, pulling her inexorably toward him.

He cleared his throat, breaking the spell he seemed to have cast over her. Nodding toward the cab door on her side, he said, "We're here."

When had that happened? Damn him. She was supposed to be distracting him. Not the other way around.

Feeling befuddled, she looked from him to the

crowded street outside her window, to the cab driver rattling off the fare. Her mind was embarrassingly sluggish, but finally she got moving.

Staying one step ahead of Ford was going to be harder than she'd thought. This was going to take some serious work.

Then just when it seemed like things couldn't get any worse, a camera flashed a few feet away. Great. Just what she needed.

Paparazzi.

Four

Ford stood near the bar, nursing a tumbler of weak Scotch, wishing he could have ordered himself a Sierra Nevada Pale Ale. He would have thought that at five hundred bucks a ticket, they could have stocked the bar with some decent beer. But of course, the best beer in the world wouldn't have distracted him from what was really bothering him. His date.

From the moment the first camera had flashed outside the hotel and she'd practically leaped from his side, she'd been avoiding him. At first, he'd assumed she just didn't want their picture taken together. That she was averting the potential scandal. But things hadn't improved since they'd made it into the event.

She'd immediately sent him off to get her a glass of

white wine and she'd been dodging him ever since. Not that he wasn't having a grand ol' time, between the event organizer who'd hit him up for a ten-thousand-dollar donation and the drunk society maven twice his age who'd been hitting on him. He hadn't had this much fun since his root canal.

Then he spotted Kitty across the room. On the dance floor. With another man. A guy who couldn't have been more than five-six and had very clingy hands.

Ford wasn't used to women blowing him off. After all, he'd only come out tonight because he'd wanted to make sure she was okay. After the near waterworks in the elevator, he'd been worried about her emotional state. Judging from the way she was laughing at Mr. Grabby's joke, she was doing just fine. But enough was enough.

He handed his drink to a passing waiter and wove his way through the crowd to the dance floor. He cut in, sweeping Kitty into his arms before she could protest. But he could tell she wanted to. As her hand settled into his, a scowl twisted her perfect features.

"I'm starting to think you're avoiding me."

"Whatever gave you that impression? After all, it's not like you wheedled your way into coming with me uninvited or anything."

He grinned at her, some of his annoyance fading at the bite of her sharp tongue. In Texas she'd been relaxed and open. Who would have guessed he'd find her bristly defenses just as appealing. "I'm a grown man. I don't wheedle."

"Hmm…" She paused as if considering her words. No doubt searching for the best way to skewer him. "How about coerce? Or maybe bully? Are those descriptions more to your liking? Are those masculine enough for you?"

He stared down at her, studying her expression. As they danced, his body brushed hers. He couldn't help remembering what it had felt like to dance with her in that bar in Texas. There, her body had melted into his; here, she held herself more stiffly. This was less a dance, more a battlefield.

"I don't like to think," he said seriously, "that I've bullied you into anything."

She arched an eyebrow. "Then perhaps you shouldn't be trying to buy my company out from under me."

"That's business."

"I thought you said it was *all* business?" she countered smoothly.

"That's not what I meant and you know it." She felt good in his arms again. Solid, yet soft. Curved in all the right places. Tempting and a little bit dangerous.

Suddenly he couldn't remember why he was supposed to leave her alone. Something about the business deal, right? It was a bad idea to mix business with pleasure. He knew that.

But Biedermann's was in serious trouble and FMJ looked like the only people stepping forward to help out. Besides, if everything went as planned, this would leave her even richer than she was now. Kitty was a businesswoman first and foremost.

But she was also a woman. A very desirable, powerful woman. He'd be an idiot to ignore the tension simmering between them. Not just because the sex would be fantastic, but because the more they tried to ignore it, the more likely it was to get in the way of business. He couldn't let his former relationship with Kitty muck up this business deal. He wouldn't let his buddies down like that.

Ford smiled. "What's going on with Biedermann's is all business. This thing between us isn't business at all."

"There is no thing between us."

Her voice was so emotionless, he almost believed she meant it. But his body had been inside hers. He'd watched her face as she climaxed. Women didn't forget that kind of thing. Sure, he could let her go on pretending they had no past, but that would just make things worse down the road if this blew up in both their faces.

"There was something between us back in Texas. I'm betting there still is."

She hesitated, her feet missing the rhythm for a moment. But then she picked up the beat again and fell into step. "You're wrong."

"And you're avoiding the obvious," he said. "You're acting like we didn't have hot, steamy sex in the back of my truck."

Her gaze narrowed into a glare. "And you're acting like a sixteen-year-old girl who put out on prom night and now wants to hear the quarterback still respects her."

He nearly chuckled at the image, but that seemed to only irritate her more.

She leaned closer to whisper vehemently, "You want to know the truth? Yes, the sex was hot and steamy. But it was just sex. Sex with a nameless, faceless stranger. It was never meant to be anything more than that. If you'd wanted a long-term relationship you should have put an ad up on one of those Internet dating sites."

"Trust me. I'm not a relationship kind of guy. I'm just not willing to be whipped. Least of all by you. Why would I? So far, you've been insulting, arrogant and generally a pain in the ass."

Surprise flickered across her face and he might have felt a twinge of guilt if every word he said wasn't true. Possibly even an understatement.

"Don't get me wrong," he continued. "It's kind of cute. In a spoiled brat kind of way."

"Cute? Spoiled brat?" She sputtered as if searching for a response. "How da—"

"How dare I? I dare because whether you like it or not, we have to work together. Whether *I* like it or not, for that matter. I thought talking about what happened in Texas might make things easier for you." Though the music continued to play, they'd slowed to the point they were no longer dancing. "Apparently I was mistaken. You don't want to talk about it? Fine. Just make sure you don't bring any of this baggage into the boardroom when we start negotiations."

She pulled her hand from his. Her gazed narrowed to a venomous glare. "Thank you for clearing that up for me. Here I was worried FMJ's offer might have been motivated by some chivalrous impulse on your part."

"Sorry, sugar." He softened his words with a grin. "I don't have a chivalrous bone in my body."

"I'm glad you've disabused me of that notion. Now I can go about being my normal…what was that phrase you used? Oh yes, pain in the ass…without feeling bad about it. That makes things much easier."

Shooting him one last haughty look, she spun on her heel and left the dance floor.

"I 'disabused her of the notion'?" he muttered to the empty spot where she'd been. "Who the hell talks like that?"

He stood there for a minute until he realized the couples around him were staring with interest. He flashed his best charming rogue smile and shrugged. "Women."

Several men tried to hide their smiles. A couple laughed outright. The women either rolled their eyes or just looked away. But he could see in their eyes that they were more amused than they wanted to be.

If the audience was keeping score, it looked like he'd won another round. It didn't feel that way, though. If only he'd believed her when she said she wasn't interested in sleeping with him. Hell, he'd even be satisfied with believing himself.

Kitty's heart pounded in her chest as she maneuvered through the maze of bodies on the dance floor. Nausea clung to her, sticky and thick. She wasn't sure how much longer she could maintain any semblance of calm around Ford. Her nerves were frayed to the point of exhaustion. Selling Biedermann's was something she'd never thought she'd consider. Just meeting with FMJ to discuss it had been abhorrent. But she'd done it. She'd dug deep to find strength she'd never known she had and she'd done the right thing for the company. And this was how fate had punished her.

Why, oh, why, did it have to be him? Why did he have to be the *F* of FMJ? Six billion people in the world and the one she never wanted to see again just happened to be the one who held her future in his hands. It was cruelty piled on top of humiliation. It was completely...nauseating.

She flattened her hand against the restroom door and shoved her way inside. The room was thankfully empty. A fact that she only had a second to appreciate before another wave of nausea washed over her. She bolted for the closest stall just as bile mixed with the rich appetizers she'd been so hungry for when she'd first arrived.

Talk about humiliation.

As if throwing up—in public—wasn't bad enough. As Kitty knelt on the bathroom floor with one hand propped on the toilet paper dispenser and the other wedged against the wall, she heard footsteps outside the stall.

"Oh, my, are you all right?" asked a wavering voice from behind her.

The voice sounded kind—benevolently maternal. Kitty wasn't taken in. Too many "kind" women were starving for gossip.

"I'm fine," Kitty managed. She raised her left leg, felt around in the air a bit for the door, then kicked it shut.

"Is there something I can get you, dear?"

Hmm…a cool washcloth? A glass of water? Retrograde amnesia? Any of the above would do.

Kitty shoved the hair out of her face and straightened, wiping at the corners of her mouth with the back of her hand.

"Perhaps I could notify your date that you're not feeling well?"

Nosy and persistent, then. Kitty stood, smoothing down her dress. In her haste, she stepped on her hem and pulled it out. But that couldn't be helped. Praying she looked better than she felt, she left the sanctuary of the stall. Kitty turned to see an elderly woman hovering by the sinks. Though she had to be nearing ninety, the woman was well-dressed and obviously took pains with her appearance.

Kitty remembered something her grandmother had often told her. There's no situation that can't be improved with a fresh coat of lipstick.

Sayings like that had made Kitty roll her eyes as a teenager. Inexplicably, Kitty chuckled. "I think I'll just freshen my makeup."

The older woman smiled. "Always a good idea, if you ask me."

Kitty faced the mirror. Her hair had lost its smooth sheen and now looked tousled beyond repair. Her face was ashen, her lips dry. Even her eyes seemed to have developed dark circles. She could only suppose they'd darkened to match her exhaustion.

And here she'd thought she looked pretty good just a few hours ago when she'd left the condo.

She sighed. By the sink there was a selection of hand lotions and perfumes, along with a bottle of mouthwash and a stack of tiny cups. She filled one of the cups with water to rinse out her mouth.

Spitting as delicately as she could, Kitty said, "This is quite embarrassing. I don't think I've ever thrown up in public before."

"Think nothing of it, dear. Every woman goes through it."

Kitty raised her eyebrows. "Every woman—" she started to ask in confusion.

"Well, not every woman. But when I was pregnant with Jake, my second, I couldn't keep anything down, either."

"Oh, I'm not… That is, I've just been under a lot of stress."

The woman gave her a pointed look. "Is that what they're calling it these days?"

"I'm not—" But Kitty's protest died in her mouth. "Pregnant."

Her vision tunneled, fading to black at the edges but staying piercingly bright in the center, where she could see her reflection in the mirror. Pale. Frightened. Terrified.

What if she was?

She couldn't be. But even as she thought it, reality came crashing back.

She was losing Biedermann's. Ford was back in her life. Running her company. So why wouldn't she be pregnant?

* * *

Ford stood in the grand ballroom of The Pierre, scanning the room one last time as the nasty truth sank in. Kitty had left him standing on the dance floor, dashed off for the bathroom and then—somehow— sneaked past him on her way out.

As unpleasant as the idea was, there was no other explanation. Kitty was nowhere to be found. Hell, he'd waited long enough for her to put in an appearance.

Maybe he had it coming. After all, this wasn't an actual date. He'd pushed his way in. Bullied her into agreeing, to use her word.

Still, he wasn't going to let her get away with this.

Forty-five minutes later, he was standing at her door, a lavish bouquet of orchids in his hands.

Her hair was loose about her shoulders, no longer sleek, but tousled as if she'd been running her fingers through it. Her face had been scrubbed clean of makeup, leaving her cheeks rosy. Her mouth was still impossibly pink, though.

She'd changed out of her dress and had a long silk robe cinched tight around her waist. The result was that she looked like one of those forties movie starlets. Somehow, even devoid of makeup and expensive clothing, she still exuded class. As if she'd been simmered in wealth since childhood and now it fairly seeped from her pores.

She eyed him suspiciously, her gaze dropping to the orchids and then back to his face. "What are those for?"

Since she didn't seem inclined to invite him in, he

elbowed past her into the apartment. "They were my excuse to get in the building. One of your neighbors was leaving. I told him I was here to apologize for a date gone bad so he'd let me in."

"And he believed you?"

"What can I say? I was persuasive."

After a moment of indecision, she closed and bolted the door. "Don't worry. It won't happen again. I'll hunt him down and kill the jerk."

"Don't do that. If you're mad at me, take it out on me." While she considered his words, he surveyed her apartment. A dingy kitchen led off from the living room and he headed there with the flowers. "Do you have a vase?"

"I thought the flowers were just a ruse."

"That's no reason not to enjoy them. Do you have any idea how hard it is to find flowers at midnight on a Friday night?"

He grabbed a vase out of one of the cabinets. It was an ornate job with elaborate curlicues. As he filled it with water, he waited for her response. She always seemed to have some snappy comeback.

It was her silence that alerted him something was wrong. He dropped the flowers into the vase and turned, thinking maybe she'd retreated to her bedroom or even left the apartment. Instead he found her sitting on the living room's sole sofa with her elbows propped on her knees and her face buried in her hands.

His nerve endings prickled with alarm.

He sent up a silent prayer. *Please don't let her be*

crying. Between his three sisters, Patrice and Suz, he'd faced down his share of weepy women.

The one thing his vast experience with crying women *had* taught him was that running like hell would only make things worse.

"Hey," he began awkwardly. "What's—"

Then Kitty stood, her eyes red, but dry.

No tears. Thank God.

She crossed to stand before him, her posture stiff with anger. "What's the matter?"

She got right in his face, stopping mere inches from him. "I'll tell you what's the matter."

She shoved a hand against his shoulder. Surprise bumped him back a step. "You are the matter."

She bopped him on the shoulder again. This time he was ready, but she was stomping forward, so he backed up a step anyway. "You come here and push your way into my company. Into my life. Into my apartment. You push and you push and you push."

With each *push* she shoved against his chest and with each shove he stepped back, trying to give her the room she needed. But she followed him step for step.

"Maybe it's time someone pushed back."

By now he was—literally—up against a wall. With his back pressed to the living room wall, he had nowhere else to go. She stopped mere centimeters away from him, her hands pressed to his chest, her eyes blazing with anger.

"I'm—" he began.

But she didn't let him finish. "Don't you dare say

you're sorry. Sorry won't cut it. *Sorry* doesn't even *begin* to cut it."

"I—"

"Well?" she prodded.

He gripped her shoulders, resisting the urge to shake her. "Stop. Interrupting. Me."

Her chin bumped up and she glared at him through stormy eyes. "Well?" she demanded again.

"I—" What?

Suddenly, he couldn't remember what it was he'd been about to say. All he could think was that this was what he'd wanted for the past two months. He wanted to see her again. To sleep with her. To strip her clothes off her, lay her bare before him in a proper bed and spend hours worshipping her body.

"'I—I—I—'" she copied, mocking his stammer. "Is that the best you can do?"

Man, she was annoying sometimes.

"No," he said. "This is."

Cupping her jaw in his hands, he shut her up the best way he knew how. He kissed her.

Five

What exactly did she have to do to insult this man? She'd sneered at him. She'd acted like a tease. She'd ditched him in the middle of their date. She'd insulted him and made fun of him. And now he was kissing her?

What was wrong with him?

Worse still, what was wrong with her?

A hot and heavy make out session with Ford was the last thing she needed right now. She wanted peace and quiet to process the events of the night. She wanted to kick Ford out of her apartment. She wanted him out of her life. She wanted to go on kissing him forever.

After months of living on memories, he was actually kissing her. Months of pretending she'd forgotten him, of believing she'd never see him again, of shoving him out of her mind during the day, but then dreaming of him when she slept. After months of waking in the middle of the night, panting, heart racing, body moist and heavy with need. After months of that, he was here. In her apartment. Kissing her.

His tongue nudged into her mouth, tracing the sensitive skin behind her lip. She shuddered, opening herself fully to him. He tasted of smoky Scotch and heat, of neediness and lust. So familiar, even though she'd only been with him once. Her body sparked to life beneath his touch.

Suddenly it didn't matter that he'd sneaked back into her life uninvited. It didn't matter that he'd deceived her. That he pushed too hard. That she couldn't intimidate or control him. All that mattered was that he just keep kissing her.

Her body remembered his touch as if it were yesterday. No matter what lies she'd told him earlier, *she* remembered. She remembered every second of their time together. As if for those few hours they'd been together she'd been more alive than at any other time in her life. As if she'd been more herself than she was in real life. The way he'd kissed her then. The cool night air on her skin when he'd kissed her in the parking lot of that god-awful bar. The heat of his hands against her flesh. The cold metal of his truck door pressed against her back.

His fingers had fumbled as he pulled her shirt over her head. She'd lost an earring. Yet when he'd touched her breasts, he hadn't been clumsy. His touch was deft. Gentle. His fingertips rough as they'd pinched her nipples, sending fissures of pleasure through her body.

He'd shoved her skirt up to her waist and his jeans had been rough against the insides of her thighs. He'd shoved her panties aside, touched her *there.* A slow, rhythmic rasping of his thumb that had driven her quietly wild. By the time he'd plunged into her, she was already on the brink of climax. The feel of him pumping inside of her combined with the chafing of his fingers had sent her over the edge.

Now, kissing him in her living room, with memories flooding her, his touch was so achingly familiar. Her body trembled with need. Moisture seeped between her legs as desire pulsed through her. She was ready for him already.

His arm snaked around her back, holding her body to his as he walked her backward, one step, then two, still kissing her. His mouth nibbled hers as if he would devour her one tiny bite at a time. And she felt powerless to stop him.

The backs of her knees bumped against the arm of the sofa just as his hand cupped her breast through the bodice of her robe. The silk provided little protection against his roaming hands, not that she wanted any. She felt her nipple tighten, hardening to his touch. Heard a groan stir in his chest.

He pulled his mouth from hers. "This isn't how I wanted this to happen."

But he poured kisses along her neck as he said it.

Proof that he was as powerless against her as she was against him.

Her hands clutched the lapels of his jacket. Pulling back, she tried to glare at him. Which was hard to do through the fog of her desire.

"How *you* wanted it to happen? What about what I want?"

He grinned wickedly, his hand flicking open the folds of her robe. Brushing the outside of her panties, he said, "I think I know what you want."

Her panties were damp with her need for him. She knew it. Maybe it should embarrass her, this desperate lust for him, the way he only had to kiss her and she went wet for him, but it didn't. Not when she knew he felt the same way. She may be wet, but he was hard. Panting. Pulsing against her hand when she ran it down the front his pants.

"You do, don't you?" Her voice came out husky. "Know what I want, I mean."

"I do."

His gaze was disconcertingly serious as he muttered the words. For an unsettling second, she considered the possibility that maybe this was about more than just sex for him. For both of them. But she shoved the concern aside.

Sex was all they had. All she wanted.

Because she couldn't think about anything else. Anything beyond this minute. This very second. She couldn't think about the mistake she might be making. Or the mistake she'd already made.

She couldn't think about the pair of pregnancy tests she'd hastily thrown out when the doorbell rang. Couldn't think about the twin pink lines on those pregnancy tests. She couldn't think about the baby already growing in her belly.

Logic told him to slow down, but she didn't let him. One minute he was merely kissing her, the next she was tumbling over the arm of the sofa, pulling him on top of her. He barely caught himself in time to keep from squashing her. He braced one hand on the back of the sofa and the other right beside her head.

For all her height, she felt tiny beneath him. He didn't want the weight of his body to pummel her. "That was close," he muttered.

"Not nearly close enough," she purred, bucking against him. Her hips rocked against his. Not in a light and playful way, but frantically, as if she were seconds from losing all control. One of her legs crept up the outside of his thigh, hooking around to anchor her hips to his.

Then she bucked against him one last time, rolling him off the sofa altogether, following him down onto the floor. Thank God for plush carpet, though even that hadn't been able to keep the breath from being knocked out of him.

Or maybe it was just her that took his breath away. Kitty. Demanding. Arrogant. Unapologetic. And sexy as hell.

She walked her hands down his chest, slowly pushing

herself into a seated position astride his hips. Her robe gaped open, barely covering her breasts as it caught on her nipples. The sash was still tied at the waist, but the robe revealed enough for him to see she was naked except for her underwear. A little scrap of fabric that felt silky and damp beneath his touch. Just kissing him had made her wet. His erection leaped at the very idea, straining against the front placket of his pants.

Head thrown back, she shifted her hips forward, grinding herself against him. She groaned low in her throat, a sound both erotic and unbearably tempting. How could he resist her? Why would he even try?

He slipped his thumb under the hem of her panties and found the nub of her desire. He stroked her there and the moan turned into a chorus of yeses. The steady chant echoed through his blood, pounding against the last of his restraint.

When she reached for his zipper, it didn't even occur to him to stop her. With a few quick movements, she'd freed him. He lifted his hips as she pulled at his pants, not even bothering to take them all the way off.

She nudged the fabric of her underwear out of the way, then lowered herself onto him. With one smooth movement, he was inside of her. Hot, tight, and unbearably sweet. He squeezed his eyes tightly closed, trying to reign in his pure lust. Sucking a breath in through his teeth, he narrowed his focus. Pleasure rocked through his body, but he stayed just ahead of it. He didn't want to come too quickly. He wanted her right there with him.

He moved his thumb in slow, steady circles, matching the rhythm of her rocking hips. With his eyes still closed, he focused on the sound of her breath, the quick gasps and low moans. The yeses had dissolved to a series of meaningless guttural sounds.

He felt her muscles clenching around him. Then he made the mistake of opening his eyes. He looked up to see her poised above him, her back arched, her breasts thrusting forward as her hands clutched her heels. With her neck arched her hair fell down her back in wild disarray. He'd never seen anything more primitive, more primal, more gut-wrenchingly erotic.

And then she focused her groans into a single word that sent him spiraling beyond control.

"Ford!"

Sleeping with Ford just about topped the list of stupid things she could have done. Ford had said she'd had a hard day and he didn't know the half of it.

And as if sleeping with him wasn't bad enough, she'd *slept* with him. When he'd picked her up and carried her to her bedroom, she'd actually tugged him down onto the bed with her, draped her body over his and promptly fallen asleep. She'd snuggled with him, for cripes sake.

When she'd peeled herself off him in the morning to sneak away for a shower, she prayed he'd at least have the common courtesy to disappear. But no. Not Ford. He made coffee.

How the hell was she supposed to defend herself against a man who'd made her coffee?

"Oh," she said joylessly. "You're still here."

"We have to talk."

"So you keep saying." She crossed the narrow kitchen to the coffeepot and poured herself a cup. "Maybe you think we're ready for couples' therapy."

He cut to the chase. "We didn't use a condom last night."

Ah. So that was why he'd stuck around.

Hoping to antagonize him into storming out, she said, "I suppose you blame me for that."

"I didn't say that. I just wanted to let you know you don't have to worry about your health. I get tested annually for anything that—"

"I know," she interrupted him. "When I got back from Texas I had myself tested. Yes, we were pretty safe, but as we both know condoms aren't one hundred percent effective at anything."

She broke off sharply. *Please don't do something stupid. Like cry. Or tell him the truth.*

"So," she continued. "I knew that wasn't a concern."

Just keep sipping your coffee. He'll leave soon and you can do all the stupid things you want.

He pinned her with a heavy stare. "Do I need to worry you'll get pregnant?"

It took all her willpower not to spew coffee all over the kitchen. Instead she equivocated. "Do I look worried?"

"That's hardly the point. You never look worried."

Well, at least she still had someone fooled. With a

self-effacing shrug, she said, "When you're raised the way I was, you learn to keep your emotions to yourself."

"Well, you learned well, then." There was a hint of something dark in his voice. Bitterness maybe, but she didn't want to consider what he might mean by that. She couldn't let herself think too much about his emotions just now.

She ignored his comment. "You don't have to worry about last night."

"You're certain?"

"Let's just say that if I got pregnant from last night, it would be a medical miracle."

Thank God he didn't press her for a more precise answer. Still, she didn't breathe deeply until he'd left and she'd thrown the dead bolt behind him.

Maybe doing something stupid like this was inevitable.

She stood in her kitchen for a long time, sipping her coffee, making excuses for her behavior. What she wanted most was to simply crawl back into bed with her sketch pad and MP3 player. To spend the whole day pretending the rest of the world didn't exist. Of course, she didn't have that luxury.

Come Monday, Ford would start pressuring her to cement the deal with FMJ. Whatever else happened, she couldn't afford to sleep with him again. There was too much at stake, for Biedermann's and for her. After all, she was going to be...

Kitty broke off her train of thought to stare down at her nearly empty coffee mug. Could pregnant women even drink coffee? Shaking her head, she dumped the last splash of coffee in the sink and washed out the mug. She'd have Casey look that up on Monday.

She paused in the act of drying the mug. Yeah, that'd be subtle. No one would ever guess she was pregnant, between puking every few minutes and having her assistant research the effects of caffeine on pregnancy.

At some point, she'd have to tell Ford about the pregnancy, but she wasn't ready for that just yet. She needed more time to process it. To figure how she felt about the tiny life growing inside of her and what it meant for her life.

She had no idea how Ford might respond to the news he was about to be a father. But she knew that whatever his reaction was going to be, she'd need to have her own emotional defenses in place before she dealt with him.

How long could she justify not telling him? A couple of days maybe. But she had to tell him and she had to do it soon.

The very thought made bile rise in her throat. She dashed for the bathroom, only to have her nausea fade, leaving her feeling queasy. The minty zing of her toothpaste helped. When she put away the toothpaste, she saw the two pregnancy tests she'd taken the previous evening.

She'd stopped to pick them up at a drugstore on the way home from the fundraiser. Her heart had pounded the whole time, sure she'd see someone she recognized. Or that at the very least someone would comment on the absurdity of a woman in formal wear buying pregnancy tests late at night. She hadn't cared. She'd needed to know.

She had still been reeling from the shock when Ford had shown up on her doorstep. He'd caught her at her most vulnerable. Again.

But it wouldn't happen a third time. From now on, she'd be prepared to deal with him. But first, she had to deal with other issues. She pressed a hand to her belly.

Logically, she should still be freaking out about being pregnant. But for some strange reason, she wasn't. Maybe some weird pregnancy hormone had been working its magic on her subconscious for the past two months. Whatever the reason, she felt strangely at peace.

Why did being pregnant have to be such a bad thing? All her life she'd dreamed of being part of a bigger family. She'd longed for sisters and brothers. How many times had she made her grandmother read *Little Women* to her? Dozens.

The only thing she'd wanted more than siblings was a real mother. Her grandmother had done her best. She'd loved her and cared for her, sure. But she hadn't done the things other mothers had done—or rather the things Kitty had imagined other mothers did. She'd never climbed onto the jungle gym at the park. She'd never built forts out of old sheets draped over the furniture. She'd never crawled into Kitty's bed to cuddle her and chase away the monsters.

Those were things Kitty's childhood had lacked. But they were experiences she could give to her child.

She could lavish this child with love. She could become the kind of mother she'd always wanted for herself. She could create the family she'd craved for so long.

What about Ford? What kind of father would he be? She bet he'd be the kind of dad who coached Little League and charmed all the teachers into rounding up his kids' grades. He'd spend too much on birthday presents, and…

Whoa. Where had all that come from? Wondering what kind of father Ford would make was the last thing she should be worrying about. It was a completely absurd exercise. Like wondering whether or not the tooth fairy was ticklish. Ford was Mr. Not-Willing-to-Be-Whipped.

There was no way he'd be interested in coaching Little League. This morning, he'd given her the perfect opportunity to tell him about the baby, but she'd balked. She hadn't exactly lied, but she hadn't told him the truth, either. And she suspected it had less to do with her mental defenses than it did with the possibility that she already knew how he'd react.

Ford wasn't looking for long term. Not with her. Not with a child. When he found out the truth, he would cut and run.

At least, dear God, she hoped he would. She could only pray he wouldn't do something noble like offer to *marry* her.

She'd been a burden all her life. For once in her life, she wanted to pull her own weight.

Yes, being pregnant now was inconvenient, what with everything that was going on at Biedermann's.

But it didn't have to be a bad thing. Not at all. The more she thought about it, the more convinced she became. She could be a good mother. She could do this. This was one dream that would not be snatched away from her.

True, she'd probably never be able to run Biedermann's the way she'd dreamed of. But being a failure as a CEO didn't mean she'd also be a failure as a mother. After all, her father had been a fantastic CEO, but a less than stellar parent. That was proof enough, if she needed it, that the two jobs didn't require the same skills. It came down to this: she'd have to be a good parent, because she was likely to be the only parent her child ever knew.

Whenever he and Jonathon traveled together, they got a hotel suite. The combined living space always made it easier to have teleconferences with Matt and to work late in the evenings. It was an arrangement that had worked well. And Jonathon certainly didn't care that Ford was returning to the hotel, having obviously been out all night. And had he slept with any other woman, Ford would have kept his mouth shut.

But Kitty was not any other woman. This morning she'd seemed fine. But the truth was, he had no idea what she was really feeling. He couldn't dismiss the possibility that he'd screwed things up. And if he had blown this deal because he couldn't stop thinking with a certain male part, then Jonathon deserved to know the truth.

"I made a mistake," he admitted as soon as he walked into the hotel suite.

Jonathan didn't even bother looking up from his laptop. A fruit plate and a bowl of oatmeal sat untouched beside his computer. "That's never a good announcement at 7:00 a.m. on a Saturday morning. But you're a big boy. I'm sure you can handle it."

"I slept with Kitty."

Jonathon's head snapped up. "Kitty Biedermann?"

"It was stupid, I know," he admitted.

A pot of coffee and a couple of cups sat untouched on the room service tray, so he poured himself a cup. He looked up to see Jonathon with a bemused half smile on his face.

"We just got here. That's fast, even for you." When Ford didn't answer, Jonathon's smile morphed into a contemplative squint. "That's not it, is it? You knew her already."

"I did. We met in Texas about two months ago." He took a sip of the coffee, relishing the heat as it burned its way down his throat. A stiff drink was what he really wanted for a conversation like this. Scalding hot coffee wasn't a bad second, though.

Jonathon studied him for a long moment, absently popping a grape in his mouth as he did. "You were the one who wanted to buy out Biedermann's."

Ford shook his head. "Biedermann's was on your list."

Jonathan stabbed a bite of cantaloupe. "Technically, that was the NYSE's list. I just referenced it when I was looking for another company to buy. There were seven or eight other companies on that list. You were the one who did all that research on Biedermann's."

Jonathon paused, chewing slowly as he watched Ford. "Unless you weren't researching the company at all. You were researching her, weren't you?"

"Look. I made a mistake. It wouldn't be the first." Ford took another drink of his coffee, wishing again it was something stronger. "I asked Wendy to find out what she could about Kitty Biedermann. She was overly enthusiastic. I didn't even know Biedermann's was on the list until you'd done most of the work."

"You should have said something then."

"I didn't think it would be a big deal. Neither of us was looking for a long-term relationship. I knew what happened in Texas was just a one-night stand and it would never happen again."

Jonathon quirked an eyebrow. "Which explains perfectly why you just slept with her a second time."

"It's not a big deal."

"So you keep saying. Are we going to have a problem with the acquisition?"

Ford thought back to Kitty's attitude. Last night she'd been passionate and demanding. This morning she'd been coolly reserved. "I don't think so," he said honestly. "She's devoted to Biedermann's. She'll do the right thing for the company. As for me, she's not emotionally involved. She's just not the boil-a-bunny type."

"How well do you know her?" Jonathon asked.

"Well enough to know that…" Then he noticed that Jonathon leaned over his laptop as he spoke, typing rapidly. Ford just rolled his eyes. "You're looking her up on Google, aren't you?" In answer,

Jonathon just shrugged. "After all the information about her that Wendy dug up, you think you're going to find something on the Internet that we didn't already know?"

Jonathon shrugged. "It never hurts."

Annoyed, Ford continued speaking. "I know her well enough to know she's not going to back out of a business deal for personal reasons."

Jonathon tapped his fingers across the mouse pad while he waited for the slow hotel wireless connection to load the results page. "I hope you're right. Kitty owns nearly sixty percent of the company. If we don't have her on board, the deal will never go through, regardless of whether or not we can convince anyone else."

"I know that." His tone was a little sharper than he'd intended.

Jonathon raised his hands in a gesture of defense. "Just reminding you." He clicked on a page, then sat back, waiting for it to load. "If she backs out now, we've wasted a decent chunk of change. And I don't like wasting time, either."

"She's not going to back out. Selling Biedermann's to us is going to make her a lot of money. That's all the incentive she needs. She's been rich all her life and we're going to make her richer. There's nothing else we need to know."

But by then Jonathon had leaned forward to read whatever Pandora's box Google had pulled up. He let out a low whistle.

"What?" Ford demanded.

"You might want to read what Suzy Snark has to say before you say anything else that'll get you in trouble."

Tension seized Ford's stomach. "Who?"

"Suzy Snark. She's a gossip blogger here in New York. Talks about Kitty every once in a while." He looked up at Ford. "You didn't really read that report from Wendy, did you? Suzy Snark was mentioned multiple times."

The tension that had started in his gut seeped through the rest of his body, leaving him frozen on the spot. He should just cross the room and take the damn laptop from Jonathan, but no matter what orders his brain issued, his feet weren't following them.

Finally he said, "Stop being so damn cryptic and just tell me what the damn thing says."

"Trust me, you're going to want to read this yourself."

He took the laptop from Jonathan and sat back down on the sofa, only vaguely aware of Jonathan walking away to give him privacy. As he read, his tension coalesced into cold, hard anger.

A few minutes later, Jonathan returned, holding out a shot of Scotch from the hotel's courtesy bar. Ford carefully set the laptop on the coffee table before accepting the drink. He took several long drinks, then realized his knuckles were turning white from gripping the glass too tightly.

Finally he stood and headed for the door with grim determination, almost too angry to speak.

"Where are you going?" Jonathan asked.

"To find Kitty."

Six

By the time Monday morning rolled around, Kitty felt marginally more prepared to face Ford. After he left her apartment Saturday morning, she'd decided she simply couldn't face him again so soon. So she'd abandoned the familiarity of her apartment for a hotel not far from Biedermann's offices. She'd spent the weekend with her phone turned off, huddled under the blanket watching an *I Love Lucy* marathon and ordering room service. She'd bawled when Little Ricky was born and then found herself unable to stop crying. Poor Lucy always tried to do the right thing, but always made a mess of things. Sometimes her own life felt like an episode of *I Love Lucy,* but without the laugh track or the comforting presence of Ethel Mertz.

Maybe this mess would seem more bearable if her own pratfalls could be cushioned by the unconditional love of her own Ricky Ricardo. Maybe if Ford…

No, she stopped herself. She couldn't think like that. He wasn't hers. He never had been and he certainly wouldn't be now that she was keeping this secret from him.

Maybe, she justified to herself, one lie of omission deserved another. In Texas, he hadn't told her that he was a business tycoon whose company was worth billions. So Saturday morning, she didn't tell him the whole truth, either.

But of course, she hadn't outright lied. After all, he truly didn't need to worry that she'd gotten pregnant then. By the time they'd had sex, she was already two months pregnant.

All of her rationalizations almost made her feel better. Until Monday morning rolled around and she found Marty pacing in her office. With his tie loosened and his hair tousled, he looked as bedraggled as she felt.

She dropped her handbag on the chair by the door and shrugged out of her coat before tossing it carelessly on top. "Honestly, Marty, have you even been home? You look as if you slept here."

Marty knew her as well as anyone did. Keeping the truth from him would be quite the challenge. Today was a day to channel her inner bitch if there ever was one.

He ignored her comment. "Where have you been all weekend? I've been trying to reach you since Saturday. We all have."

Kitty's stomach tightened. This didn't sound good. "I went away for the weekend." Another lie. Sort of.

What could she possibly have done wrong now? She hadn't even been here. Running his fingers through his hair again, Marty asked, "Have you been online this morning?"

She faked a yawn to cover any panic that might have crossed her face. "You know I can't stand staring at a computer screen before coffee. Speaking of which, could you be a dear and get—"

"No, Kitty. Not this morning." He rounded her desk and popped open her laptop. "Come have a look."

By the time she reached it, the Suzy Snark blog was loading onto the screen. At the top of the page was a picture of her and Ford climbing out of the cab in front of The Pierre Hotel. Whatever nasty comment Kitty had been about to make was swallowed by her dread.

She stared blankly at the screen, her eyes unable to focus on the jumble of words on the screen. After a second, she realized Marty was looking at her expectantly.

"Well," he said.

She dropped petulantly into her office chair. "Why should I care what some gossipmonger has to say?"

"You should care because it affects your business."

"I sincerely doubt it."

"Are you even going to read it?"

You bet your booty she was. But not now, with Marty looming over her, watching the painful process. "Maybe later. After coffee."

Marty twisted the laptop to face him and began reading aloud. "Christmas has come early for those of us who love juicy gossip—"

"Honestly, Marty," she interrupted. "Is this really necessary?"

"Yes." His tone was unexpectedly firm. "You need to read this before anyone from FMJ shows up."

She mimicked his tone. "Fine. Then be a dear and get me that mocha latte and I'll be done reading it by the time you get back."

As soon as he was gone, she leaned forward and began the laborious process of reading.

Christmas has come early for those of us who love juicy gossip. Readers of this column are probably wondering why Kitty Biedermann's love life has been so dull lately. Ever since her breakup with Derek Messina, she's been nursing her broken heart in private. But no longer!

This time she's set her sights on entrepreneur Ford Langley of FMJ. The two were seen together at the posh Children's Medical Foundation fundraiser just last night. It's not surprising the enterprising Kitty would try to land such a hunky catch. The shocker is that they may be entering into professional negotiations as well as personal ones. There are rumors that Biedermann's is about to get gobbled up by FMJ.

And that's not even the biggest news. An inside source says Kitty may be expecting more than just a hefty bonus from FMJ. The only question is, once Langley finds out about Kitty's little bundle of joy, will he still be interested in saving Biedermann's Jewelry? Or will the heiress have to raise her baby and run her company all on her own?

Kitty felt bile rise in her throat as she sat back in her chair. Oh, dear lord.

Before she even began to ponder the issue, Marty reappeared. The mocha latte he set down in front of her did nothing to settle her stomach. His stony expression did little to quell her fears.

"I got a decaf. Just in case she's right." He must have read her answer in her expression, because he propped his hip on the edge of her desk and muttered a curse. "How did she find out?"

"I don't know," she admitted.

"Guess."

But she couldn't guess. She'd known herself for less than seventy-two hours. How had Suzy-stinkin'-Snark found out about it?

"I bought a pregnancy test," she said aloud. "Someone must have seen me do it."

Marty sighed. "And if it was someone who reads the blog and recognized you, they would have contacted Suzy right away."

Marty's obvious annoyance rankled. "Why are you acting all put out over this? This is my private life she's exploiting."

"And it affects our business. Why were you out with Ford anyway? Did you think making a conquest of him would make this buyout any easier on you? Do you really think FMJ is going to want to do business with you when you act like this?"

She could only stammer in response. For years she'd put up with Marty's passive-aggressive kowtowing, and now—the one time she could have really used him in her corner—he was turning on her?

Kitty was saved from having to formulate a defense when Ford appeared at the door.

"Oh, goody," she muttered. "Because I wasn't feeling beleaguered enough."

Ford swept into the room with all the subtly of a tsunami, and he brought flotsam and jetsam in his wake. Jonathon and Casey followed him.

"I assume you've both seen it."

Kitty opened her mouth to answer, but before she could, he turned to her assistant. "We're going to have to make a preemptive strike. We'll schedule a press conference. But not for this afternoon. We want to appear proactive, but we don't want to lend credence to the blog by appearing to be reacting to it. So announce the press conference, but schedule it for a few days out. Wednesday maybe. Jonathon, why don't you and Marty get started on that? Casey, you can—"

Fear propelled her to her feet. "A press conference?" She tried to scoff convincingly. "Over a piddling gossip blog? Isn't that overreacting?"

Ford turned the weight of his gaze on her. He crossed his arms over his chest. "Not at all. FMJ's acquisition of Biedermann's hasn't been officially announced yet. It doesn't look good that the news was leaked."

Right. The acquisition. The news of her pregnancy had overshadowed everything else. She'd forgotten that the blog even mentioned the buyout.

"But," she protested. "It was leaked to a *gossip* blog. One that no one is likely to read. And it's even less likely that anyone who does would care about business."

"This blog may have a wider readership than you think. We all read it within a few hours. We have to assume others have, too. If we work fast, we can minimize the damage."

"Why should we respond at all? We certainly don't want people thinking that whatever this woman posts online is true."

Marty's gaze had been ping-ponging back and forth between them. Ford narrowed his gaze at the other man, giving him a why-are-you-still-here look. Before Marty could respond to the unspoken question, Jonathon ushered both Casey and Marty out with such practiced ease, she couldn't help wondering if he and Ford had orchestrated the move.

"Wow," she murmured. "I'm impressed. Normally it's impossible to get Marty out of my office when he's got a bone to pick." She gestured between Ford and the door through which Jonathon had just vanished. "Did you guys plan out that two-pronged approach? Not that I mind. If we have to talk about that blog, I'd much rather do it without an audience."

"Damn right we have to talk about that blog. Was she right? Are you pregnant?"

* * *

"Does it matter?" Kitty countered smoothly.

Her lack of denial was all the confirmation he needed. Ford gritted his teeth against the questions he wanted to throw at her. As prickly as she was, it wouldn't take much to push her into a full-fledged argument.

"I'd prefer a quiet wedding, but I'll leave that up to you. We should—"

She spun to face him. "We're not getting married."

"Of course, we're getting married." A hard note crept into his voice. "I'm not going to desert my family."

For a long moment, she seemed to be considering him. Then she patted her belly with exaggerated care. "Well, lucky for you, this baby and I aren't your family."

Kitty stood there, one hand propped on her hip, chin up, all defiant bravado.

"You're saying it's not mine?"

"I'm not *saying* it isn't yours. It *isn't* yours."

"But you are pregnant?"

Her chin inched up a notch. "What I am is none of your business. Not your burden. Not your problem."

"You couldn't be more than a couple of months pregnant," he pointed out.

"What's your point?"

"The timing is perfect for me to be the father."

She quirked an eyebrow, her expression full of arrogance. "What, you think I came back from Texas so satisfied that I couldn't even imagine being with another man?"

"I suppose I would like to think that. But the truth is, you're not the type to sleep around."

"Oh, really?" she asked, her voice brimming with challenge. "And you're such an expert on me? How long have you known me, Ford, really? A week? It's less than that, isn't it? The truth is, you have no idea what I'm capable of."

If she was lying, she did a damn good job of it. There wasn't so much as a sputter of doubt in her eyes to give her away.

He waited for the surge of relief. Pregnant or not, she was letting him off the hook. All he had to do was take her at her word and walk away.

He studied her standing there, taking in the defiant bump of her chin, the blazing independence in her eyes. She was dressed in slim-legged pants and a fuzzy sweater that made her look touchable. But that was the only hint of softness about her, otherwise she was all hard angles and bristly defenses.

Kitty was pregnant. There was a baby growing inside her belly. A tiny life. Maybe his. Maybe not.

But his gut said it was his. Every possessive, primitive cell in his body screamed that her child must be his.

Of course, that didn't mean it *was*.

"You're right," he said finally. "I don't know you well, but I'm a good judge of character. I know you well enough to know you're capable of lying to get what you want. The only thing I don't know is what it is you want."

She squared her shoulders and met his gaze. "What I want is to save Biedermann's. If FMJ can do that, then we'll have a deal. If not, I'll find someone else who can."

* * *

"Are you sure you don't want Marty here?" Ford asked as he sat down at the conference table. "He is your CFO."

"I'm sure." They were working late, trying to get all the details of the acquisition hammered out before the press conference later in the week. Thanks to Suzy Snark, they needed to work much faster than they might have otherwise. Instead of sitting herself, she stood near the windows, staring out at the cityscape below. Marty made her so damn nervous. She'd asked Ford to set up this meeting between him, her and Jonathon precisely because she couldn't ask the kinds of questions she needed to with Marty in the room.

Of course, Jonathon made her nervous, too, with his steady gaze and his brilliant head for numbers. He was exactly the kind of person who made her feel twitchy with fear. But Jonathon couldn't be avoided. She no longer trusted herself to be alone with Ford.

Which was why she waited until Jonathon had settled into a chair at the conference table before speaking.

"If I'm going to hand my family's company over to your tender care—" Kitty stressed the words *tender care*, letting them hear her doubts that their management of Biedermann's was likely to be either tender or careful "—then I need assurances that you actually have a plan in place."

Jonathon cleared his throat. "If you've read the proposal we sent, you'll see your compensation package is—"

Ford interrupted him. "I don't believe it's her compensation package she's worried about."

She looked over her shoulder, surprised by his comment. He sat at the table, leaning back in his chair, one ankle propped up on the opposite knee. The posture was relaxed, but there was an intensity to his gaze that made her breath catch in her chest.

"Yes." She forced fresh air into her lungs. "Exactly."

Now, Ford sat forward, steepling his hands on the table before him. "Unless I'm mistaken, Kitty is the rare CEO who is less worried about what she's going to get out of this settlement than how the company is going to be treated." He pinned her with a stare that she felt all the way to her bones. "Am I right?"

In that instant, the intensity of his gaze laid her bare. All the artifice, all her defenses, the image she'd worked her whole life to build and maintain seemed to vanish like a whiff of smoke, leaving her with the disconcerting feeling that he could see straight through to her very soul.

"You are," she said simply.

"I don't understand." Jonathon frowned, looking down at his laptop as if he expected it to sprout flowers. "Why did you ask to meet with us alone if you weren't worried about your end of the deal?"

"I thought you'd be more honest in private." Which was also true and was as good an excuse as any. "I don't care how much money I walk away with. I don't care what kind of golden parachutes you offer to the board members. I care about whether or not the stores themselves survive. When this is all over with, is there going to be a Biedermann's in nearly every mall in America? Are there going to be any of them left?"

The question hung in the air between them. Since they seemed to be waiting for her to say something else, she continued.

"If FMJ gobbles us up, that may solve the immediate problem of our declining stock prices, but that's only part of the problem." She turned to Jonathon. "Our stock price wouldn't be going down if we had strong retail performance. I want to know how you plan to improve that."

She expected Jonathon to answer. After all, he was FMJ's financial genius. However, it was Ford who spoke.

"You're right. For too long, you've been relying on people shopping at your stores because they're already at the mall. However—"

Ford broke off as his cell phone buzzed to life. Reaching into his pocket, he grimaced as he pulled out the phone. "Sorry."

He turned off the volume on the phone, but left it sitting on the conference table by his elbow. "It's not enough…"

Even though he continued talking, her attention wandered for a second. She'd seen the name displayed on the phone when it rang. *Patrice.* What were the names of his sisters? Chelsea, Beatrice and…something else. Certainly not Patrice, though.

Not that it mattered in the least. He probably had the numbers of dozens of women stored in his phone. Hundreds maybe. It wasn't her business.

She forced her attention back to his words.

"We don't want shoppers to stop in at Biedermann's because they're at the mall. We want to attract them to the mall because there's a Biedermann's there. We need Biedermann's to provide them with services and products that they can't get anywhere else."

"We have strong brand recognition," she protested. "We offer more styles of engagement rings than any other store."

"But engagement rings are a one-time purchase. You need something that will bring customers back again and again."

The phone by his elbow began to vibrate silently. Again she glanced down. This time the name display read Suz.

"You can answer it if you need to," she said.

He frowned as the phone stopped vibrating and the call rolled over to voice mail. "I don't."

"Are you sure? Second call in just a few minutes."

Jonathon was scowling, clearly annoyed. He quirked an eyebrow in silent condemnation when the phone started vibrating again a few seconds later. Rosa this time.

Was that the third sister's name? She couldn't remember.

"Just answer it," Jonathon snapped.

Frowning, Ford stood as he grabbed the phone. "Hey, miha. What's up?" With a slight nod, he excused himself from the room.

For a long time, Kitty and Jonathon sat in silence, the tension taut between them. She suspected he didn't like her any more than she liked him. With his frosty demeanor and calculating gaze, every time she glanced at him she half expected to see little dollar signs where his pupils were.

However, after a few minutes of drumming her nails against the armchair, her patience wore out. Or perhaps her curiosity got the better of her.

"Does he always get so many personal calls at work?"

Jonathon scowled, but she couldn't tell if he was annoyed by the interruption or by her questions. "It's after hours. But his family can be quite demanding."

"Those were all family members?" Maybe she'd misremembered the names. Or perhaps misread them?

Jonathon's scowl deepened. Ah, so he hadn't meant to reveal that.

"I know he has three sisters, but—"

"If you're curious about his family, you should really talk to Ford about it."

And let him know she was scoping out his potential as a father? Not likely.

She met Jonathon's gaze and smiled slowly. "The problem, Mr. Bagdon, is that whenever Ford and I are alone, we end up doing one of two things. Neither of them is conducive to talking about his family."

Mr. Cold-As-Ice Jonathon didn't stammer or blush. Instead, he held her gaze, his lips twisting in an expression that she might have imagined was amusement in a man less dour.

"Interesting," he murmured.

"What?"

"You expected me to be either embarrassed or distracted by your honesty."

"But you're neither?" she asked. What was it with these guys from FMJ that none of them reacted the way normal men did?

"Certainly not enough to be tricked into telling you the information you're fishing for."

Well, if her motives were going to be so transparent, then she might as well be honest. "Very well, then. Let's be frank. I am curious about Ford, but I don't want to ask him about his family."

"Because…" Jonathon prodded.

She smiled. "If there's one thing you and I can both agree upon, it's that the relationship between Ford and I is complicated enough as it is. Yes, I could talk to him about it, but I wasn't merely being provocative with my earlier comment. Every time Ford and I are alone we're either fighting or having sex. I don't see any reason to add emotional confidences into an already volatile mix merely to satisfy my curiosity."

Jonathon studied her for a moment, his expression as nonplussed as it always was. Finally he nodded. "Very well. What do you want to know?"

What didn't she want to know might have been a better question. Ford seemed such a dichotomy. She thought of the easygoing charmer she'd met back in that bar in Texas. He'd seemed such a simple man. Not stupid by any means, but uncomplicated. It was that quality that had drawn her to him in the first place. With his laid-back charisma and magnetic smile, he'd coaxed his way past her defenses as easily as he'd mollified Dale.

That alone should have made her suspicious. A man that could assess and defuse a tense situation like that was no mere cowboy. Far more telling was the way he'd charmed her. She never let down her defenses. Never let anyone close. She should have known that any man who could tempt her into a quickie in the parking lot was a man to be reckoned with.

What was that saying? Fool me once, shame on you; fool me twice, shame on me.

Well, she was suitably shamed.

Regardless of all that, Ford—this chameleon of a man, whom she barely knew and couldn't possibly hope to understand—was the father of her child. She had no way of anticipating how he would react if he were to learn the truth.

She clearly took too long to formulate her question, because Jonathon leaned forward. "If you've got a question, you should ask now. He might not be on the phone with his family much longer."

Suddenly, she was struck by an awful thought. Her skin went clammy as panic washed over her. Dear God, what if the reason Jonathon didn't want to talk about Ford was because he was married? Choking down her dread, she asked, "By family, you don't mean wife, do you?"

Jonathon laughed, a rusty uncomfortable snort of

derision. "Ford? Married? Hell, no. He's that last man on earth who would cheat on a wife."

She clenched her jaw against her innate dislike of being laughed at. "Well, I hardly know him. How am I supposed to know that?"

Jonathon's smile faded. "Ford's father kept a mistress for the last fifteen years of his life. He had a whole other family he had set up in a house one town over. While he was alive, he kept all those balls in the air himself. But when he passed away, he'd named Ford executor of his will. All of sudden Ford had to find a way to make peace between these two families."

"My goodness. What did Ford do?" She asked the question almost without realizing she'd done it.

"Ford did what he always does." Jonathon's expression had turned from icy to grim. "He smoothed things over."

Okay, so she wasn't exactly an expert on women, seeing as how most of her friends were men. She could only imagine how she would feel if she found out that the man she'd loved had had another family secreted away somewhere. She'd be pissed. No amount of "smoothing things over" would make that all right. And yet, if anyone could do it, she believed Ford could.

"They must just hate each other," she murmured.

"Surprisingly, they don't." Jonathon shrugged as if to say he didn't get it, either. "They resented each other for a long time, but now they're friends, strange as that sounds. Ford's younger sister—his full sister, that is—

Chelsea is about the same age as Beatrice. Ford managed to convince both Suzanne and Patrice that the girls all needed each other. Of course, it helped matters that his dad had died practically broke. So Ford was pretty much supporting everyone."

"How old was he?"

"Twenty-three or so."

She'd read somewhere that he'd made his first million by the time he was twenty-two. If he was supporting five women not long after that, he must have been highly motivated indeed to keep making money. From what he'd told her, his sisters were only now in college.

She glanced toward the door to her office through which Ford had disappeared. "This kind of thing, with the constant phone calls. This happens often?"

"Only when there's some crisis they want him to solve. They tend to…um, disagree a lot. When they do, they all call Ford to sort it out for them."

"So he solves all their problems, but he never lets them get too close, does he?"

Jonathon sent her a piercing look. "Why do you say that?"

"Because it's what I would do."

Seven

From where she sat, she could see Ford through the open door of her office. He stood with his back toward them. Tension radiated from him. She could see it through the lines of his shoulders, in the way he shifted them as he spoke, as if he were trying to stretch out the knotted muscles. But she could hear the tone of his voice, as well. Not the words, the tone. Quiet and soothing.

She wondered, did his family know he was lying to them? If not with his words, then with his intent.

She was watching Ford so closely that Jonathon surprised her when he said, "You say that because you think you're so much alike."

There was the faintest hint of condemnation in his

voice. It made her chuckle. "Oh, God, no. Not at all."
Finally she looked back at Jonathon. "He's so
charming, isn't he?"

"I don't know what you mean."

"I saw it in Texas. The way he can manipulate
people. Talking them into things. Get them to do things
they normally wouldn't."

"You're saying he charmed you into bed with him."

She slanted a look at Jonathon, tilting her head to
the side as she studied him. "Do you always do that?
Willfully misunderstand what people are saying?"

"I've found most people say things they don't really
mean. And mean things they're not willing to say
aloud. I've found it's best to make sure everyone is on
the same page."

She nodded. "Very well, then, maybe he did charm
me into bed with him. But I certainly wasn't unwill-
ing, if that's what you were asking. No, what I meant
was that he has the ability to charm everyone. But I
don't think he lets many people close."

No, like her, he kept everyone at arm's length. His
charm was as much a weapon as her sarcastic quips. She
couldn't say exactly why she knew that to be true, simply
that she understood it on a gut level. The same way she
knew that if fate hadn't thrown them together again, she
never would have seen Ford after that one night in Texas.

Somehow the thought made her sad. Ford wasn't
hers to keep, but she was glad she'd had this chance to
see him again. To get to know the man he really was.
Even if that man wasn't someone she could let too close.

Jonathon didn't respond, but studied her with that same steady gaze she found so disconcerting.

"Have I satisfied your curiosity?"

Kitty flashed him a cavalier smile. "You've certainly answered all of my questions."

More to the point, he'd told her everything she really needed to know about Ford. If he found out he really was the father of her child, he'd do everything in his power to take care of her. But he'd never really let her or the baby in. He'd never love her or the baby the way she wanted to be loved. She'd just be another burden to him.

And wasn't that just the last thing she needed? Another man to coddle her. Yippee.

Ford couldn't tell how much progress he and Jonathon had made on convincing Kitty to accept their offer, but he sensed something had changed while he'd been on the phone with his sister. He'd come back to the table to find Kitty looking pale and withdrawn. To make matters worse, not much later, Jonathon had gotten a call, as well, and had to leave the meeting.

Now half a day had passed and they were no closer to signing papers. Kitty had vanished after lunch, leaving him to go over the quarterly financial statements with Marty, whose eager nervousness reminded him of a puppy with ADD.

To make matters worse, he'd wandered over to Kitty's office. He hadn't planned on coming there. That's just where he'd ended up. As if he no longer had any control over where his feet took him.

A quick glance in her office told him it was empty. She better not have left early. He'd already turned to leave when he heard a noise from the other side of the office. The door to her bathroom was open.

"Kitty, are you there?" he asked, crossing her office.

He was a few steps from the bathroom when the door slammed closed. "Go away," said her muffled voice.

He should have taken at her word, but he made the mistake of hesitating just long enough to hear the recognizable sounds of someone throwing up. He cringed.

"You okay?"

"Go a—" More retching.

That sounded bad. Not that hurling ever sounded good. He should definitely leave. He'd almost made it to the door when a voice in his head stopped him in his tracks. *She's obviously sick, and you're running for the door. What kind of jerk are you?*

But she'd told him to go.

Of course she did. No one likes puking. You think she's going to ask for your help? No way. But you can't just leave her there.

He walked back to the bathroom, praying the door would be locked. That would be the perfect excuse to just turn and walk away. He tried the knob. And the damn thing wiggled.

He opened the door to see her wiping her mouth with the back of her hand. Thick strands of dark hair had fallen down from its twist to hang in her face. Her gaze blazed with anger.

"I said go away." But her hands trembled as she lowered herself to sit on the ground beside the toilet.

He'd done the right thing.

Shutting the door behind him in case anyone came in, he said, "You don't have to be so proud."

"Great. A lecture. Thanks." She pressed her cheek to the tile wall. "Next time you're throwing up, I'll fly out to California to razz you."

"Yeah, I'll give you a call," he shot back. He pulled a paper towel from the dispenser and ran it under the faucet before handing it to her. "Here."

"Thanks." She wiped carefully at the corners of her mouth, then folded that edge to the center and pressed the damp cloth to her forehead. A sigh of relief escaped her lips.

The sound stirred something deep within his belly. Some primitive urge to care for and protect. To possess.

Okay, she should not look sexy right now. That was just wrong.

He looked around for something else to do and saw a mug sitting on the ledge under the mirror. After rinsing it carefully, he filled it. He squatted by her side and held it out.

After a second, her eyes flickered open. She stared at him for a moment. If she saw the heat in his gaze, she didn't comment, but the tension seemed to stretch between them as she sipped the water. He half expected her to come back with one of her customary jabs. Instead she said merely, "Thanks."

"You're welcome. Can I get you anything else?"

"One of my lollipops. Top drawer of my desk. Right-hand side."

Glad to have something to do, he headed straight for her desk. The first thing he saw when he pulled out the top drawer was an artist's sketchbook. A large pencil drawing dominated the page. In the bottom left-hand corner was a scared little girl in a pinafore dress, with black curls and huge eyes, like a cross between Shirley Temple and Betty Boop with just enough Kitty Beidermann thrown in to make the character unmistakable. She clutched her hands in front of her in exaggerated terror. Behind her loomed an enormous monster, all pointy teeth and glistening drool. Its arms arched over her head, wicked claws gleaming. The monster's body was formed by the letters *F, M* and *J*. The overall effect was both humorous and compelling.

So, she fancied herself an artist, did she?

He grinned as he picked up the sketchbook and flipped the page. However, the other pictures weren't cartoons but rather sketches of jewelry. It was the same tongue-in-cheek, gothic sensibility, but applied to intricate drawings of necklaces and earrings.

"Find one of the yellow ones, if you can," she called out from the bathroom.

He looked back in the drawer and saw a pile of lollipops. After digging through for a yellow one, he headed back to the bathroom, flipping through the sketchbook as he went.

When he reached the bathroom, he tucked the book

under his arm to pull the wrapper off the lollipop. He held it out to her. "These help?"

She plopped it in her mouth and rolled her eyes at him, either in relief or at his obvious doubt. After several strong sucks that caved in her cheeks and worked her throat in a way that was alarmingly erotic, she nodded.

"They're specially formulated." She spoke between sucks. "High in Vitamin C. Sour flavor. Helps with the morning sickness."

This was morning sickness? Undeniable proof of the baby growing in her belly. The baby that was maybe his, maybe not his. But she was definitely making herself known. He felt as if a hand reached into his chest and gave his heart a squeeze.

Kitty swayed a bit, apparently still feeling wobbly, and he automatically reached out a hand to steady her. Her touch on his arm felt weak and trembling. That hand squeezing his heart tightened to a fist.

Before she could protest, he wrapped one arm around her shoulder and gripped her arm with the other, guiding her out of the bathroom to the sofa in her office.

They'd just left the bathroom when her door opened and Marty strolled in. He stopped dead in his tracks, looking from Kitty and back to Ford, then to the open bathroom door through which they'd obviously just walked. Together.

Marty's gaze narrowed and his cheek muscles twitched into a frown. "I'm glad with all the work we have to do that you two are finding ways to amuse yourselves."

Ford waited for Kitty to explain her morning sickness. Instead she pressed her body against his side and slithered her arm around his waist. With exaggerated slowness, she pulled the lollipop from her mouth and smiled. Then she slanted him a look meant to turn men rock-hard.

"Me, too," she murmured with the faintest wink.

Marty gave a disgusted squawk and fled the room, apparently imagining that they were about to go at it again right in front of him.

As soon as the door shut behind him, Kitty sprawled on the sofa, stretching her legs out in front of her indelicately and popping the lollipop back in her mouth with absolutely no artifice.

"Oh, thank God he's gone. Like my nausea wasn't bad enough without having to listen to him."

"You could have explained."

"Trust me. The last thing I need is Marty feeling sorry for me." She shuddered with mock disgust, closing her eyes again to concentrate on her lollipop.

Her hand rested on her belly, her fingers absently toying with the swatch of knit that covered the exact spot where he imagined her baby growing. The way she'd stretched across the sofa, her belly appeared perfectly flat with only the gentlest slope to her stomach. No one would guess she was even a day pregnant. She must not be very far along. More than a month, since she'd already taken the test, but not much more. Maybe two.

The recesses of his brain started doing a little involuntary math, but he shoved the thought aside. She'd said it wasn't his. She was letting him off the hook. That was enough. He didn't want to be a dad and he sure as hell didn't want to inflict himself as a father on any poor kid. It wasn't just him she was letting off the hook. It was all of them. Until she was far enough along to get proof one way or another, he had to take her word for it anyway.

To distract himself from those disconcerting thoughts, he pulled the sketchbook out from under his arm and started flipping through it again.

"What is this?" he asked.

She opened a single eye to gaze at him. When her gaze fell on the sketchbook, she tensed for a second. Then she closed her eye and forced a breath that almost sounded relaxed. "Just doodles."

"They don't look like doodles. They look like jewelry designs."

He held up the page to reveal a sketch of a necklace and earrings. The set was full of intricate curlicues and elaborate swirls in a style that managed to reference Victorian styles while still looking modern.

"It's just something I drew up. It's not even very original."

"What do you mean?" He turned the page to look at the next design.

"I modeled it after some of my grandmother's old jewelry. The ones I had to sell. Most of the drawings in there came from pieces of my grandmother's. A swirl here, a flower there. Just bits I combined together from one piece or another."

He looked up from the drawings. Her free hand still rested on her stomach, but her fingers had started tugging at the knit. Normally Kitty's innate confidence bordered on arrogance. If he didn't know better he'd think she was fidgeting.

He flipped to the next page, staring at the image for a moment before turning the page ninety degrees to get a better angle. "Is this a case for an iPhone?"

She pulled in her legs, straightening. "You know not everyone likes their gadgets to look like gadgets."

It was the same scrolling design as one of the earlier pictures, but this time the perfect size and shape to enclose a cell phone. The page held three drawings, one of the back; the second depicted elegant, tiny, clawed feet, which wrapped around the front of the phone; the third showed the delicate hinges along the side. He could imagine it in gleaming sterling. The overall effect was a brilliant merging of gothic Victorian and geeky tech. Between the clawed feet and the ghoulish tiny gargoyle face on the back, the piece almost had…a sense of humor.

Like the drawing of FMJ gobbling up Kitty.

"Did you think of this?" he asked.

"It's similar to my great-grandfather's cigarette case."

"Wait a second." He flipped back a few pages to the drawing of the earrings and pendant. He squinted at the scrawled writing he'd dismissed initially. In tiny letters he saw the words *Bluetooth?* and *ear buds?* "This isn't jewelry, is it? These are gadgets. This isn't a necklace, it's a case for an MP3 player."

She reached to pull the sketchbook from his hands. "You don't need to poke fun at me."

"I'm not." He held the book just out of her reach. "I think it's brilliant."

Her gaze narrowed in suspicion as she stepped closer to him, still reaching for the notebook. "It's completely unrealistic."

"Says who?" he asked.

"Everyone I've ever showed it to."

"Which is?"

"My father. The board of directors. No one's gonna buy geeky jewelry."

He scoffed, dismissing her concern. "Let me guess. Your father was one of those guys who thought iPhones would never sell, either."

She set her jaw at a stubborn angle. "Besides which, Biedermann's *sells* jewelry, we don't make it." Once again she reached for the notebook. "We don't have the means or the experience to even do a mock-up of that kind of thing, let alone manufacture it."

"Biedermann's doesn't." He thumbed through the pages until he returned to the first image that had caught his attention. He flipped the book around to display the picture of FMJ. "But FMJ does." He grinned. "Sometimes it's good being the evil monster."

She blinked in surprise, then chuckled for a second. But then she studied his face, finally pulling the sketchbook from his grasp. "It's too risky."

"No, it isn't. Matt has a whole electrical engineering department that would love to take a whack at this. Let me just fax him a couple of the pages."

"No."

"But—"

She turned on him suddenly. "Biedermann's is practically hemorrhaging money right now. The absolute last thing we need to do is venture into something like this. If we took a risk like this and it failed, we'd never recover."

"Then the trick is not to fail."

"That's so easy for you to say. Everything you touch turns to gold, right? Buy a company, sell a company. It's all the same. You make millions in your sleep. Besides, if you're wrong, and Biedermann's dies off completely, you can still sell off chunks of us to recoup some of your losses. FMJ could probably use the tax write-off anyway. It may not matter to you whether or not Biedermann's flounders or flourishes, but it matters to me."

As gently as he could, he said, "You know, Kitty, for someone who claims to be desperate to save Biedermann's, you're sure not willing to take many risks to do it."

"I am willing to take risks. I'm just not willing to risk everything."

A second later, she'd snatched her purse out of the desk and was gone. And, damn it, she'd taken her sketchbook with her. He was going to have to find a way to get it back, because he was going to send those drawings to Matt. This could be the key to everything. The niche market Biedermann's was looking for. Not just upscale jewelry, but high fashion accessories for the gadgets nearly every American owned.

Biedermann Jewelry. It's not just for engagements anymore.

He nearly chuckled at his own little joke. This could really work. Between Matt's electronic genius and Kitty's artistic brilliance, they could hit a market that no one else had tapped. Biedermann's would be back on top. And best of all, Kitty would be responsible for that.

He could do this for her. He could fix her professional life.

God knew there wasn't much he could do for her personal life.

Eight

From the blog of New York gossip columnist Suzy Snark:

> Fiddling while Rome burned. Polishing the brass on the Titanic. Both phrases imply great negligence in the face of disaster. New Yorkers may want to add a new idiom to that list: Getting a massage while your company is being bought out.
>
> I know, we usually eschew the nitty gritty business details for outright gossip, but this tidbit was too salacious to keep to myself. Besides, the business geniuses at FMJ have scheduled a press conference for this afternoon to announce their acquisition of Biedermann Jewelry. I thought

you might want something to consider while they're trying to convince their stockholders it's a good thing they're squandering their own resources to bail out Ford Langley's girlfriend.

Readers will be shocked to learn that while Biedermann Jewelry stock prices continue to plummet, heiress Kitty Biedermann continues to receive daily spa treatments. Sources say she spends upward of two thousand dollars a week on mani-pedis and facials. In a time when her personal finances must be taking a hit, that's got to hurt.

Is the heiress addicted to pampering? Is she simply careless? Or is there something else going on here? Perhaps she sold all her Biedermann stock back when it was still worth something. Too bad she didn't see fit to tip the rest of us off, as well.

"Is any of this new blog true at all?" Ford asked.

She glanced at the image on his iPhone. Her stomach clenched at the sight of the scarlet swirl at the top of the screen. Another Suzy Snark blog. Just what she needed.

"Ah," she quipped, trying to sound completely blasé. "Suzy Snark. What fun."

"Have you read it?"

"I don't read trash."

He held out the iPhone. "You need to read this."

Panic clutched her stomach. Her gaze darted from the phone to his face. She wanted nothing to do with any of that rubbish.

"Why don't you try to sum it up for me?" she suggested in her best spoiled-brat voice.

"It accuses you of negligence." Ford continued to hold out the phone as if he expected that to be all the encouragement she needed.

Though her heart seemed to stutter in her chest, she didn't reach for the phone. What exactly had Suzy Snark discovered?

Ford continued, his tone full of exasperation. "She says you've been spending your days at the spa. Getting massages and pedicures when you should be working."

"Is that all?" Her heart started thudding again, a rapid tattoo she was sure Ford would be able to hear.

"What do you mean 'is that all?' Is there more?" he demanded. "Is there something you're not telling me?"

Instead of answering, she tried to sidestep the question. "It's just a stupid gossip blog. You and Jonathon place entirely too much importance on what this woman writes. What does it even matter?"

He shoved his phone back in his pocket. "It matters. It may just be a gossip blog, but who knows how many people read it. This woman maligns you every chance she gets. Has it occurred to you that Suzy Snark may be the reason Biedermann's stock is in free fall?"

She sucked in a breath. "No. It hasn't."

"I did some preliminary research. Every time she posts about you, the stock price dips. Starting with today's press conference, we're going to defend you against this woman's lies. Now why don't you—"

But he must have seen the truth in her expression,

because Ford broke off. He studied her in silence for a moment before slowly shaking his head. "She's not lying, is she?"

"I wouldn't know. I didn't read the blog."

Ford ignored her comment. "Is she right? Have you really been spending hours of every workday at the spa?"

"I'm not going to defend myself to you."

"You're going to have to defend yourself to someone. The fact that you haven't denied any of this makes me think it must be true."

"What is it you want me to admit to? Going to the spa sometimes? Fine, I do that. Every woman I know gets regular manicures and pedicures. Most men I know, too. It's not a crime."

"No. But if you're doing it during office hours, every day, then it looks bad. It looks like you're not doing your job. It looks like you don't care about the company. And if you don't care about it, then why should anyone else?"

"Is that what you think? That I don't care about Biedermann's? I would do *anything* for Biedermann's."

"So you keep saying. But, frankly, I'm not seeing it."

"Are you kidding me? Since I took over as CEO, I've poured everything I have into this business. I've spent every waking moment trying to educate myself on how to be the best CEO I can. I've listened to every damn business book published in the last decade, from *Barbarians at the Gate* to *The 4-Hour Workweek,* none of which have been remotely helpful, by the way. I've worked eighty-hour weeks. I've abandoned my social life completely.

"None of that made any difference. The stock price just kept going down. So I decided to buy whatever stock I could in hopes of keeping the price up. I liquidated all of my assets. Sold everything I had. Furniture, art, jewelry. Things that had been in the family for generations. I quietly auctioned it off piece by piece. A year ago, I moved out of the townhouse where I grew up, where Biedermanns had lived for over a hundred years. I sold it and moved into a *walk-up*."

To her embarrassment, her voice, which had been rising in pitch steadily, broke on the word *walk-up*. She knew where she lived was the least of her worries, but somehow it signified all the things wrong in her life.

Knowing she was being ridiculous didn't make it sting any less when he said, "Come on, you make it sound like life without a doorman just isn't worth living. Surely it's not that bad."

"Have you ever lived without a doorman?" she asked.

"I live in a craftsman remodel down by campus in Palo Alto," he deadpanned. "I've never had a doorman in my life."

"Well, I now live on the fourth floor in a building without an elevator. I grew up with staff, for cripes sake. Our housekeeper worked for my family for forty-five years. After I let Maggie go, she couldn't even afford to pay the tuition for her granddaughter's college."

Maggie had been like family. No, more than that. To a girl who'd never known her mother, Maggie *had been* family. And Kitty had had to fire her. Sweet Maggie had tried to comfort her, made her hot tea and murmured optimist platitudes like, *I've always wanted to travel.* Maggie had been too proud to accept a handout once she was no longer employed, so Kitty had done the only thing she could do. She'd tracked down Maggie's granddaughter and hired her at Biedermann's.

"Then why did you sell the house?" Ford was asking her. "And if you had to sell it, why not move someplace nicer?"

At his question, she bumped her chin up defiantly.

"Because," she shot back. "When the stock price started to drop, I couldn't just stand by and do nothing. So I bought as much as I could. And then when it kept dropping, I couldn't even pay the taxes on the townhouse. Selling the house was the only option."

"You should never have invested your personal assets in—"

"I know that, okay?" she snapped. "I was trying to help Biedermann's and I made a stupid mistake. I'm really good at making stupid mistakes, thank you very much."

It was just one of many, many stupid mistakes. Sometimes she felt buried under the weight of them.

"I'm just trying to—" he began.

But she cut him off with a belligerent glare. "I don't need your help."

He talked over her protests. "If Biedermann's really does go under, you'll have lost everything."

What could she say to that? All she could do was shake her head and blink back the tears. "If Biedermann's really does go under, then I've lost everything anyway."

But that wasn't entirely true anymore, was it? She'd have the baby. She'd have the family she'd always wanted. It was a small consolation that was turning into everything.

"So tell me this," he said. "If you're so desperate to keep Biedermann's afloat, why this elaborate act? Why don't you want anyone to know what you're doing? Why spend your days at the spa getting massages and facials? You've got to know how bad that looks."

She met his gaze. "I can't—" she began before breaking off. Then she swept a hand across her forehead, pushing her hair out of her face. "I can't explain that."

"Well, try. Make me understand what's going on here. Give me something, anything, that makes this make sense."

"This is just what I do."

Whenever the influx of written material got too much to handle, she took Casey, went to the spa and had her assistant read aloud to her. The paperwork was so overwhelming. Business documents were the worst. She just couldn't wrap her head around the pages and pages of words. Listening to them read aloud helped. But what kind of CEO had her assistant read everything aloud? Christ, it was like she was a preschooler at story time. How could she explain that to Ford?

Instead she said, "It's like a…a coping mechanism or something."

"You mean the massages are a way of relieving stress?"

She all but threw up her hands in frustration. "No. I mean, I was raised never to reveal my weaknesses. You always have to keep up appearances."

"I don't understand."

"No. Of course you wouldn't. My mother died when I was young. My father was completely loving and indulgent, but Biedermann's always came first, so he wasn't around a lot. I was raised by my grandmother, who was already well into her sixties when I was born. It…"

She struggled for words. Finally she finished with, "It made for an unusual upbringing. I grew up in the 1990s, but really, it's like I was raised in the 1950s. To my grandmother, appearances were everything. I know she loved me, but in the world she lived in, you never let anyone see your weaknesses. You never aired your dirty laundry."

And a child with a disability—a child who was imperfect—was the ultimate dirty laundry. She'd been such an embarrassment to her whole family. Such a disappointment. How could she stand disappointing anyone else?

"So, going to the spa is your way of whistling in the graveyard? Of pretending everything is okay when it obviously isn't? You're not fooling anyone."

"I fooled you, didn't I?"

"You didn't fool me so much as make me doubt your sanity." His words were like a slap. He must have regretted them, because he sighed and scrubbed a hand down his face. "Look, you've got to defend yourself against Suzy Snark's allegations. Whoever she is, you've got to let people know she's wrong about you."

"And tell them what? That I was completely unprepared to take over as CEO? That I have no discernible leadership skills? That I have nothing to offer the company at all? How would admitting any of that help matters?"

"At least people would know you cared," he said finally.

Then she sighed, suddenly exhausted by the conversation. "My pride is all I have left."

For someone who'd lived her life in the public eye, Kitty seemed surprisingly nervous during the press conference. He doubted that anyone in the press noticed.

They stood side by side, along with Jonathon and Marty, a united front against the questions of the press. After he'd made the initial speech about FMJ's decision to acquire Biedermann Jewelry, Jonathon had stepped forward to outline the basis of FMJ's financial plan for Biedermann's.

As Jonathon spoke, Ford stopped listening. It was all stuff they'd discussed before. Instead he focused his attention on Kitty. She stood beside him, dressed in a gray pin-striped dress that wrapped around her waist. It managed to mimic the feel of a business suit, but its curve-hugging lines looked outrageously feminine. Her hair fell in dark, glossy waves, shadowing one side of her face. Bright red lipstick highlighted the bow of her lips. She looked like she'd stepped out of a Maxim photo shoot. A teenage boy's idea of how a woman should look in the workplace. A sexpot in a business suit.

Probably every man in the audience was mentally undressing her.

Hell, he wasn't a teenager and even his body had leaped in response to the sight of her. He'd had to battle some primitive urge to drape his jacket around her shoulders and bundle her back to her office, where he could strip her dress from her body and worship her like an acolyte.

At least until he'd noticed how nervous she was. Outwardly, she seemed fine. More than fine, actually. The press no doubt saw the confident, beautiful—if a little overblown—woman that she intended for them to see. That he'd seen at first glance.

It was only at second glance that the illusion began to slip. Her smile, though open and alluring, was a little stiff. It was too unwavering. There was no play about her lips.

This wasn't just nerves. This was perfectly contained, well-schooled nerves. This was someone who spent a great deal of time and energy learning to hide her panic.

The idea that Kitty—so composed, so polished and poised—might be fighting panic knocked him off balance. So off balance, in fact, that he let the press conference go on much longer than it should have.

Before he knew it, there was a blond reporter who looked about twenty-two saying, "Ms. Biedermann, when your father died unexpectedly last year, you were obviously woefully unprepared to take over as CEO of

Biedermann Jewelry. Can you explain why you insisted on serving in a position you have neither the skill nor the training to hold? And furthermore, how do you answer allegations that it's your gross incompetence that has led to Biedermann's current predicament?"

Ford kept waiting for Kitty to interrupt the reporter. Sure, Kitty was obviously nervous. But he'd seen the subtle signs of nervousness from her on other occasions in which she'd gone on to cheerfully lambaste him.

From what he'd seen, Kitty never backed down from a fight and never took crap from anyone. So he was blindsided when the reporter made it past the phrase "woefully unprepared" without getting the verbal equivalent of a body slam. Why wasn't Kitty defending herself?

By the time he heard the phrase "gross incompetence" he was done waiting for Kitty to don her own boxing gloves. He stepped up to the microphone. "If there are any signs of gross incompetence, I haven't seen them. FMJ would not have invested this kind of money in a company whose leadership we questioned."

"Then is FMJ merely investing in Biedermann's?" a different reporter asked. "Or can we expect you to do your signature restructuring and complete overhaul?"

"We'll be announcing some very exciting things for the stores soon." He flashed his best charming smile. "I promise you this, within a year everyone in this room will be shopping at Biedermann's."

"And about rumors that this acquisition is fueled by a romantic relationship between you and Ms.

Biedermann?" This question was again from the annoying blond.

Ford shot Kitty a glance to see if she was finally going to light into the woman, only to see Kitty still had that deer-in-the-headlights look.

So he ducked his head and gave the reporters his most boyishly mischievous smile. "Well, you found me out. This is all just a ruse to ask Kitty Biedermann out on a date. I figured a techie geek from California like me wouldn't have a shot with a blue blood like Kitty Biedermann. Hell, I couldn't even get her to return my phone calls before." A chuckle rumbled through the audience of reporters. "But seriously, my relationship with Ms. Biedermann is purely professional. On my first night in town she took pity on me and allowed me to accompany her to the Children's Medical Foundation fundraiser. We attended as business colleagues."

"So you're not the father of her baby?"

"Ms. Biedermann's personal life is a private matter. Let's keep this about business."

And with that, Jonathon took the cue to wrap up the press conference. A few minutes later, Ford guided Kitty out the room and whisked her up to her office. By the time he had her alone, his shock had given way to anger.

"What the hell was that?" he asked even as he slammed the door shut behind them.

She spun around, her eyes wide. "What?"

"The way you behaved out there with the press. That's what."

"I don't know what you mean," she stammered.

She pressed a palm to her stomach as if to still the fluttering in her belly. He grabbed her by the wrist and held her hand out between them. "Look at you. You're shaking."

She jerked her hand away and thrust it behind her back. "So what if I am? Those things make me nervous."

"Yeah. I noticed. But that's no excuse for letting that reporter walk all over you."

Kitty glared at him. "What was I supposed to do?"

"You were supposed to defend yourself."

"How could I defend myself? She was badgering me with questions. There was nothing I could do."

"Kitty, I've watched you go toe-to-toe with a drunken rancher twice your size. Hell, every time we meet you try to rip me a new one. You know how to hold your own in a fight. That ninety-pound reporter shouldn't have had a chance."

She turned away, obviously searching for an explanation that would placate him. Finally she said simply, "That reporter was telling the truth."

"About us?" he asked. "We agreed what happened between us is nobody's business but our own. If you had a problem lying in a press conference, you should have told me that before—"

"Not about us," she interrupted. "About me." Again she turned away from him, but this time he sensed it was because she couldn't bring herself to meet his gaze. "All those things she said about me were true."

"Kitty—"

"About me being 'woefully unprepared.'" There was a disparaging sneer in her voice. "About my gross incompetence. It's all true."

He stared at the stiff lines of her back, barely comprehending her words. She looked like someone waiting to be hit.

For a moment he could only stare at her while he sorted through his confusion. "What do you mean? You're not incompetent."

"You only think that because I do such a good job hiding it. But I don't know what I'm doing. I wasn't prepared to run Biedermann's. The board never should have named me CEO."

"Kitty, being a CEO is a difficult job. People are rarely prepared for it. In your situation it was worse because your father's death was so unexpected and you were grieving for him. I'm sure it feels overwhelming. But that doesn't make you incompetent."

She glanced over her shoulder, sending him a watery smile. Where those *tears* in her eyes?

"You're not listening to me. No amount of preparation would have been enough. I'm just not smart enough."

And then he made his biggest mistake. He laughed.

She flinched. Exactly as if she'd been slapped. She was facing the windows again, so he didn't see her expression, but he would bet those tears were spilling down her cheeks by now.

He wanted to cross the room to her, take her in his arms and offer her comfort, but he knew that stubborn pride enough to know she wouldn't want him to see her crying. He wouldn't add insult to injury by making her face him.

"Kitty, I'm sorry, but the idea that you're not smart is ridiculous."

"Ford—"

"I've listened to you verbally skewer just about everyone you talk to. You can work a crowd like no one I've ever seen. Anyone who can hold their own in a room full of wealthy socialites could not possibly be stupid. If you weren't smart, believe me, I'd have noticed by now."

She shot him an exasperated look. "Why are you arguing with me about this? When my father and grandmother were still alive, they protected me the best they could. When my father died unexpectedly, I should have had the sense to step aside. But I was selfish. I love this company more than anything. I thought that would be enough. But I only made a mess of things."

She seemed so dejected, so unlike her normal self, he reached out a hand to her, but she deftly slipped out of his reach.

"You mentioned at the press conference that you'd be doing some restructuring. If you really intend to do everything in your power to ensure Biedermann's is financially viable, then you'll fire me."

Nine

"What the hell is up with Kitty?"

Ford cornered Casey looking for some answers. Casey glanced up from the pot of coffee she was making just as Ford shut the door to the break room.

Casey slanted him a look from under her shaggy bangs. "Do you mean, like, today? Or ever?"

The previous times he'd spoken to Casey, she'd impressed him as being little more than a surly reprobate. He'd wondered how such a girl had gotten a job at Biedermann's, let alone kept it. Nevertheless, the best way to get the dirt on someone was through his or her assistant. Besides, she seemed to be the only person Kitty might confide in.

So Ford flashed Casey a sympathetic smile. "Kitty must be pretty tough to work for, huh?"

The girl's characteristic frown darkened to a full-fledged glower as she shoved the coffeepot onto the heating element and flicked the on/off toggle. "If you're just looking to talk trash about Kitty, you'll have to find someone else. I'm not into that kind of negative bonding. This job's too important to me."

He held up his hands in a gesture of innocence. "I was just trying to be sympathetic."

"You were just trying to dig for information," Casey said shrewdly as she pulled a clean coffee mug from the cabinet.

"Maybe I was," he admitted, more than a little surprised by Casey's show of loyalty. Since the negative bonding Casey had accused him of obviously wasn't going to work, he decided to take a different tack. "Kitty's not always the most forthcoming person. I'm trying to figure her out. That doesn't make me the enemy."

Casey shot him a suspicious look, but said nothing as she poured cream and then sugar into the mug. She sent an equally dark look at the coffeemaker, which was gurgling slowly. Poor girl was obviously torn between her need for caffeine and her desire to storm out in a huff.

"I'm trying to help her. But I can't do that unless I understand what's going on. Something's—"

"You're trying to get her fired."

"I'm not." Hell, that was the last thing he wanted. Keeping Kitty employed and well taken care of would at least minimize his guilt. "I'm trying to save her job. But she's not giving me anything to work with. She's—"

"She's too proud," Casey said quietly, without meeting his gaze.

"Exactly." Encouraged by the lack of belligerence in Casey's tone, he pressed on. "Do you have any idea why she would think I should fire her?"

"She said that?" Casey's voice held a note of panic.

Wasn't that interesting. "You're really worried about her losing her job."

"Hey, I know what people around here think. That she's such a b—" Casey broke off and seemed to be considering the hazards of cussing in front of the man who was ultimately her boss. "Such a witch—" she corrected "—to work for that I'm the best she can get. But it's not like that."

Ford said nothing. He'd wondered himself how exactly a surly, semicompetent girl like Casey had landed a prime job like the assistant to the CEO of a major company.

"She's the best boss I ever had," Casey continued. "And if I lost this job, I'm guessing I'd lose the scholarship, too."

"The scholarship?"

"Yeah. The scholarship that pays tuition for community college for all Biedermann employees. 'Cause there's no way I could pay for college on my own. I'd have to drop out of HCCC."

"Oh. That scholarship."

He'd read just about everything on Biedermann company policy, and he'd never heard of an employee scholarship. Which made him think Kitty was paying for this girl's college out of her own pocket. Kitty, who'd had to sell her home and had auctioned off family heirlooms, was paying the tuition of this ill-mannered, unskilled girl.

Was Kitty...*softhearted?* It was easier to imagine the Dalai Lama sponsoring an Ultimate Fighting match.

But what other explanation was there?

He shoved a hand through his hair. Damn it, why did she have to be so full of contradictions? Why did she have to be fragile one moment, all bristly defenses the next? Why couldn't she just be the manipulative witch that everyone thought she was? That would make his life so much easier.

If he ever wanted to be free of Kitty and all the complicated emotions she stirred up, he was going to have to find a way to save Biedermann's. And save Kitty's job.

And apparently Casey's job, too.

"Look," he said to Casey. "I'm trying to do the right thing here. Not just for the company, but for Kitty, too. If you help me out, if you help me understand what's going on here, I'll make sure you don't lose your job. Or your scholarship."

Even if he had to start paying the girl's tuition himself. And wouldn't that be just great. 'Cause all he needed in his life was one more woman dependent on him.

Casey pursed her lips and studied him. "What do you want to know?"

"Kitty told me her father never expected her to run Biedermann's. Do you know why?"

Casey shook her head. "No. I never met the old man, 'cause I was hired after he died. But office gossip is he always wanted her to marry someone who'd take over as CEO. You ask me, it's why that skeezie Marty is so mean to her."

"You think Marty expected to be made CEO?"

She shook her head, pouring coffee into her mug now that the maker had finally stopped dripping. "Haven't you noticed that icky way he looks at her? Like she's his golden lottery ticket or something. I think he wanted to marry her himself." Casey jabbed her coffee with a spoon and gave it a brisk stir. "That guy creeps me out."

Ford felt a sucker punch of jealousy. He struggled to bury it. Kitty's love life wasn't his business. Or so he kept telling himself. Still, he found himself asking, "Did she and Marty ever go out?"

That was not him giving in to his curiosity. If Marty was smarting from a broken heart, that might be motivation enough for him to make things unpleasant for Kitty. He might even be leaking information about Kitty to Suzy Snark.

"Naw." Casey waved her hand, dismissing the possibility. "Kitty wouldn't stoop that low." But then Casey tilted her head to the side, considering. "But Marty isn't, you know, smart about women. And you know what Kitty's like. Marty might have thought she was hitting on him."

Ford had to stifle a groan. Yes, he did know what Kitty was like. She used her beauty and sensuality like a defensive shield. Whenever someone got too close, she'd turn into Kitty the vamp. Had she accidentally hit Marty with that overblown charm of hers? Had she crushed his expectations, and somehow turned a man who should have been her friend into an enemy?

"Ah, Kitty," he murmured half under his breath. "Maybe you really are stupid."

Beside him, Casey stiffened. "Hey, that's just mean."

"No, wait," he jumped in to correct her. "I didn't mean—"

"She's not stupid, she's dyslexic, and if you don't know the difference then you're the idiot."

"She's dyslexic?" Ford barely heard Casey's words as shock spiraled through him.

Dyslexic? Kitty was dyslexic?

"She hides it well, right? I guess when you have a disability like that, you're used to dealing—" Casey broke off and did a visible double take. "Wait a sec. You didn't know?"

Guilt flashed across Casey's face, but then she turned and scurried from the room, cupping the mug in both hands, shoulders hunched defensively.

What did he even know about dyslexia? He'd gone to high school with some kids with dyslexia, one of whom had gone on to become a rather famous jazz musician. Ford hadn't kept in touch with Steve, but they'd been friends in school and he remembered how much trouble Steve had had learning.

Suddenly Ford remembered things Kitty had said or done that hadn't made sense before now. In all the meetings they'd been to together, whenever someone handed out information, she'd never even look at it. Proposals, contracts, synopses, whatever. She'd just slip it into her leather folio without so much as a glance. Her behavior gave the impression of careless disregard for the work of others. But that wasn't it at all.

And what was that she'd said once? Something about listening to books about business. Not reading them. Listening to them.

If she had trouble reading, her job would be nearly impossible. Add to that the possibility that she may have inadvertently offended her CFO.

He thought about his own relationship with Jonathon. At FMJ, he, Jonathon and Matt functioned more as a triumvirate than their titles would imply. Still, he'd be unable to do his job as CEO without Jonathon. Their relationship and their success stemmed from their absolute trust.

No wonder Kitty was floundering as the head of Biedermann's.

Ford broke into a quick jog to chase after Casey, who was now halfway down the hall. "Hey, hold up."

Casey rounded on him, her expression hardened into protective defiance. "You can't say anything to her about this."

"Of course I'm going to talk to her about it."

"You can't," Casey pleaded in a whisper. "If she finds out I told you, she'll fire me! She's totally crazy about hiding it. I'm not even supposed to know."

"Then she didn't tell you herself?"

"No way." Casey sent a furtive glance down either end of the hall as if she expected corporate spies to be lurking around every corner.

"So you figured it out on your own."

"Yes." Casey started walking again, apparently satisfied that no one was listening in on their conversation. "Like, my interview for the job was a dead giveaway. She didn't care if I could type or use a computer or anything. She just had me read aloud. And that's pretty much my whole job. Every time she goes to get her nails done or to get a massage, she has me come along to read to her."

Which explained why Kitty spent so much time at the spa. What had she called it? A coping mechanism.

He remembered what she'd said about how appearances were everything. No wonder she didn't want anyone knowing she had a learning disability. Unfortunately all the things she'd done to protect herself ending up making things worse.

Casey sent him a pleading look. "You're not going to tell her all of this, are you?"

"I have to."

He felt like he finally understood her. He only hoped it wasn't too late to help her.

Just when Kitty thought her day couldn't get any worse, Ford showed up at her apartment. Again.

She stood with her hand on the edge of the door,

glaring at Ford through the foot-and-a-half gap between the door and the jamb. "Let me guess, some idiot in the building let you in again."

"It was a different guy this time. But he'd watched the press conference and I convinced him we really were in love and just didn't want anyone to know it."

"What is it with you sneaking into my building?"

"It's nothing personal. I just didn't think you'd let me up."

"I wouldn't have. Probably because I didn't want to see you. Funny how that works, isn't it?"

She couldn't really blame her fellow tenants for being unable to keep Ford out of her building when she couldn't keep him out of her mind. He was a charming bastard, that was for sure. She'd always thought of herself as an expert at manipulating men. So why was it none of her tricks worked with him? Worse still, why was his persistence so appealing?

That was the real problem. Not that he wouldn't leave her alone, but that she didn't want him to. She moved to shut the door in his face, wishing she could block out her feelings as easily.

But he blocked her with his foot in the door. "Why didn't you tell me you were dyslexic?"

Her stomach clenched at his words as a wash of chilly panic flooded her. How had he found out? It was a secret she'd kept her whole life. The one she'd done everything to protect. She'd been prepared to resign from Biedermann's rather than talk about it. And he'd found out anyway.

Damn him. Why couldn't he just stay neatly in her past the way one-night stands were supposed to? She shoved aside all her emotions, burying them deep in her belly, pretending they didn't rise up in the acid of her sarcasm.

"Why didn't I tell you I was dyslexic?" she repeated. "The question is, why would I? It's completely irrelevant and frankly no one's business."

He reached out a hand as if he were going to pull her into his arms, but she deftly avoided his grasp. She'd been staying one step ahead of intimacy her entire adult life. Why should he be any different?

He clenched his jaw, staring her down with his hands propped on his hips. His very body presented a formidable line of offense. "You should have said something."

"I hardly even notice it," she lied, moving to the far end of the room before turning and circling back. "You have a birthmark on your shoulder. We've never talked about that, either."

"I wasn't about to resign over my birthmark."

"Well, maybe you should," she said glibly. "It's hardly your best feature."

"Stop it."

She stilled, taken aback by the edge in his voice as much as his words. Glancing around, she realized she'd made a complete circuit of the living room and now stood before him once again. She was back where she'd started.

Sometimes her whole life felt like that. As if she was

going in circles, always moving, always pretending she was making progress, but never getting anywhere.

Tears burned her eyes as she felt her throat close off. God, she would not do this. She would *not* cry in front of him.

It was bad enough when she'd done it at the office. When she'd had the excuse of the stress of the press conference to fall back on. She wouldn't do it again.

She tried to move past him, to just keep moving. As she always did. Because moving in circles was better than standing still, even if she wasn't getting anywhere.

But he snagged her arm as she walked by. He turned her to face him. "You don't have to pretend this doesn't matter to you. You don't always have to be so tough."

She laughed; it sounded bitter and unpleasant even to her ears. "You can't possibly understand what my life has been like. Do you have any idea how many people would love to see me fail?"

He studied her for a minute, clearly considering her words. "Have you ever considered that there might be just as many people who'd like to see you succeed?"

She blinked, surprised by his words. But he was wrong. Stubborn, but wrong. "You don't know what you're talking about."

"I know enough," he continued, "to know that people with dyslexia aren't stupid. And that there are plenty of dyslexic people who are very successful."

"There may be. But I'm not one of them." He looked like he wanted to say something, but she glared at him defiantly. "Don't."

"What?"

"Don't try to sugarcoat this. You never would have before you knew about my disability."

"I wasn't about to—"

"Yes, you were. I could see it in your eyes. You were about to tell me that it's not my fault that Biedermann's is in this situation. Or worse still, that things aren't as bad as they seem. Because I know better. *You* know better. If Biedermann's wasn't circling the drain, FMJ wouldn't be here, offering to buy us out. If things weren't desperate, you wouldn't be here at all. And trust me, the last thing I want is for you to treat me differently now that you know I have a disability."

"Okay," he said slowly. "I won't lie to you. Things are bad." He stroked a soothing hand down her arm. It was a gesture that was benignly gentle. Paternal, almost. "But that doesn't necessarily mean you're responsible. Businesses fail for a variety of reasons. You're not—"

"Yes, I am. I'm the company's CEO. That means I'm responsible. Biedermann's has thrived for five generations. Until I took over. And for the past four quarters we've released negative earnings and our stock is plummeting. If FMJ were in the same situation, you wouldn't flinch from taking responsibility yourself."

"Maybe you're right." He stroked her arm again in that maddening way. The touch was generically tender. As if he was gentling a horse or comforting a child. As if knowing she was dyslexic made her less desirable. "If you don't think you can serve as CEO, then we'll find something else for you to do. Your sketches were amazing. You could launch your own line of jewelry."

His words stirred up a long-buried yearning. Her own line of jewelry. It was what she'd always wanted. Her barely acknowledged greatest dream. His words might have even placated her, if she didn't know just how impossible that dream was. He was leading her on just to appease her vanity. Worse still was the way he stroked her arm.

His touch was so completely innocent, so totally sexless, it sparked her anger. She was more than her dyslexia. She wasn't a child. She wasn't a spooked animal. She didn't need to be comforted or soothed or reassured.

"Stop that." She jerked away from his touch.

"What?"

"That thing you're doing where you stroke my arm. With that calming, gentle touch." She propped her hands on her hips and glared at him.

"What is it you want from me, exactly? You want me to admit how hard this is on me?"

"That would be a start." There was a note of surprise in his voice. As if he hadn't expected her to cave so easily.

"Of course, it's hard. Biedermann's is ingrained in my family. My father and grandparents always took so much pride in the company. This is what people in my family have been doing for five generations. Ever since I was a child, running Biedermann's was all I ever wanted to do."

"Surely it wasn't what you always wanted."

"Of course it was," she snapped; for an instant her irritation edged out her softer emotions. "My father brought me to work with him from the time I was a toddler. You know, I never missed having a mother." She turned away, embarrassed by the confession. Afraid that it made her sound heartless. Or worse, that it was a lie. That she truly *had* missed having a mother. That if her mother had lived, Kitty might have been a completely different person. More lovable. Her natural defensiveness kicked in and when she spoke her tone was bitter with resentment. "My father loved me enough for two parents. I had the best of everything. I went to the best schools. And when those weren't good enough, I had the best tutors. He coddled me all my life. Maybe that's why it was so shocking when I found out the truth."

To her surprise and embarrassment, her voice broke on the word *truth*. She brought her hand to her cheek and felt the moisture there. She brushed fervently.

Before she could hide them, he was suddenly at her side. With a gentle touch of her shoulders, he turned her to face him. She swallowed past the lump in her throat, resisting the urge to turn away from him.

"What truth?" he asked gently.

"That I'd never be able to run Biedermann's. That I'd never be more than just a pretty accessory." Through the sheen of her tears, she saw the flicker of disbelief. "He'd taken me out of school and hired private tutors. He carefully regulated everyone I came into contact with. He was only trying to protect me, but it meant I had no idea what I was capable of. Or rather incapable of. I was in college before I knew how odd my upbringing was. Before I realized I was reading at a third grade level and I'd never graduate. In *college*." She let out a bitter bark of a laugh. "I hate to think how much money he had to donate to get me in in the first place."

Tears streamed down her face. She looked up at him, fully expecting to see the panic most men displayed when faced with tears.

But there was no panic. No terror. And he wasn't running away. Instead, he leaned down and brushed a gentle kiss across her lips before he pulled her close and wrapped his arms around her.

She sank against him, relishing his strength, even as it annoyed her. She didn't want to want him. She wanted nothing more than to be left alone with her misery. But apparently he wasn't going to let her do that. And she wasn't strong enough to make him go away. Not when she had such a short amount of time with him anyway.

When he leaned down to take her mouth in a kiss, she met him, move for move. She pressed her body against his, needing the feel of his muscles moving beneath her palms.

His hands moved over her body, peeling away layers of clothing as easily as he'd stripped away her emotional defenses. He swept her up into his arms and carried her to the bedroom as effortlessly as he'd swept back into her life. His every touch heightened her desire.

She needed him. She needed this. Here, in the bed, they were equals. A perfect match.

With him, she could be herself as she could with no one else. But as much as she wanted this moment to last forever, she knew it couldn't. Her heart filled with bittersweet longing, even as he made her body soar. Even as pleasure shuddered through her nerve endings, she knew it was the last time they'd ever be together.

She had to tell him the truth about the baby and once she did, everything between them would change forever.

Ten

"This wasn't what was supposed to happen," she murmured.

Boy, she'd said a mouthful there.

"Ain't that the truth?" he muttered.

She pulled back just enough to look up at him. Through a sheen of dried tears she gazed into those liquid brown eyes of his and felt some cold icy part of herself melt.

Finally he asked, "What was supposed to happen?"

"You were supposed to leave." She ducked her head back to his chest.

"I was?" He tipped her chin up and studied her expression. "Is it so bad that I stayed?"

She let out a sigh that was part tearful shudder, part

exasperation. Her lips curled in a wry smile as she answered. "Yes, it is."

"I don't get it." His smile held both humor and something darker. "I know why I *shouldn't* stay, I just don't get why you don't want me to."

"Think highly of yourself, don't you?" She stretched as she said it, arching against the wall of his chest, relishing the feel of his strength. "But I can't argue with that at all," she continued. "In bed we're great together. It's out of bed that we're a disaster."

As easily as she'd slipped into his arms, she pulled herself free. The tears were gone, but her eyes felt dry and scratchy, as if she'd bawled for hours.

"You think we're a disaster together only because this thing with Biedermann's is between us," he pointed out.

"Not only because of that," she murmured, grabbing her clothes, but didn't explain.

"Not only. But mostly."

She bumped up her chin. "Even with only Biedermann's between us, that would be enough. The company is my whole life."

"True," he admitted. "But we're not on opposing sides here. You keep treating me like the enemy, but I'm not. FMJ is here to help. We're here to fix things for you."

"That's just it. You don't see anything wrong with that, do you?"

"With what?"

"The fact that you want to fix things for me." The fact that she had to explain it at all was only more proof of the problem. "That you want to help."

"No, I don't. It's what we do at FMJ. It's what *I* do."

"Exactly. If I let you, you'd swoop in and take over everything for me. FMJ would manage Biedermann's and I'd never have to make another decision in my life. Just sit back and live off my stock dividends and never worry about anything ever again."

"Most women wouldn't be complaining about that," he pointed out wryly.

She thought of what Jonathon had told her about his mother and sisters. Maybe they were content to live like that, but she never would be. "I think you're wrong about that."

"Look, you said yourself you were raised to find a rich husband, marry him and let him run Biedermann's for you. How is what I'm proposing any different?"

"For starters, you're not actually proposing, are you? It's different when people are married. You're suggesting a business arrangement. Out of pity, no less."

"Fine," he said, an unexpected bite of irritation in his voice. "You want to get married? We'll get married."

For a second, she just stared at him in shock. What did he expect her to do? Leap with joy? Instead, she let out a bark of laughter. "You want to marry me so I'll feel better about accepting money from you? That's ridiculous."

"Why? Because you're too proud to accept help?"

"No. Because people should get married because they love each other, not out of some misguided sense of…" She searched around for the right word, before finally pinning him with a stare. "Why exactly did you propose again? Was it pity?"

"It was *not* pity." He returned her gaze steadily. "Did you love Derek?"

"I…" That had been different. With Derek, it had been all business. Not this crazy mixture of business, lust and emotion. "That was different."

"How?"

"I could trust him." At least, she'd thought she could trust him. More to the point, she could trust herself with him. She knew how she felt about him. She admired Derek's business sense and his ambition, but she never could have loved him. When he dumped her, he'd wounded her pride, but her heart hadn't felt the slightest hiccup.

Quite simply, she'd never loved Derek, but she did love Ford. With him, it would be totally different. She'd be so vulnerable. She'd be at the mercy of her own emotions. And he would treat her just like he treated everyone else. He'd be charming, thoughtful and solicitous. Without ever actually caring about her at all.

Of course, she couldn't say any of that aloud. So instead she said, "And I understood his motives."

"I just thought—" Ford broke off, struggling to put into words what he could barely understand himself. "Look, you're pregnant. The single-parent thing is really hard. I watched Patrice struggle to do it for years. And Mom, after my dad died. It's a tough gig." He must have read the absolute horror on her face, because he let his words trail off before finishing lamely, "I don't know. I thought, maybe I could help out with that."

"Wow," she began with exaggerated disbelief. "You thought that *maybe* you could 'help out' raising your own—" And then she stopped dead as she realized what she'd just said. "You should just leave."

"What was that you were going to say? Raising my own *what?*" He grabbed her arm as she reached for the doorknob. "My own what? My own *child?* That's what you were going to say, wasn't it?" He searched her face, but she'd quickly schooled her expression to reveal nothing. "Wasn't it?" he demanded.

She yanked her arm from his grasp. "I misspoke."

"No, you didn't. You know that baby is mine. Tell me the truth."

Kitty met his gaze, chin up, eyes blazing. "I have no idea who the father of this baby is. Yes, I slept with you, so it could be yours. But I sleep with a lot of men. It could be anyone's."

He just shook his head. "You little liar."

"You don't believe me?" she asked coolly.

"Not for a minute. Saturday morning, when I was worried because we didn't use a condom, you told me you'd been tested when you got back from Texas. But we had used a condom in Texas. There was no reason for you to think you might have picked something up from me. Unless you were just being incredibly careful. Which you wouldn't be unless what happened in Texas was rare. Like, once in a lifetime rare."

An odd mixture of frustration and relief washed over Ford. *Why the hell hadn't he thought of this earlier?*

It was so obvious now that he'd thought it through. No one else could be the father of her child, because there was no one else. For Kitty, there was only him.

And he didn't even want to think about how much better that made him feel. How that strange pressure in his chest started to ease up. All he knew was this: he was the father of Kitty's child. Now she had to marry him. There was no reason not to.

"We're getting married," he announced. "That's final."

"That," she sneered, "is the stupidest thing I've ever heard. Getting married because I'm pregnant may actually be more stupid than getting married because you feel sorry for me."

"I'm not going to fight with you about this."

"Good, because I'm not going to fight with you about it, either. You can't make me marry you. You want to support the baby. Fine. Send a check. If you even want to be a part of the baby's life, I'm okay with that. We'll negotiate custody or something. But I'm guessing you won't even want that."

Fury inched through him, slow and insidious. Because she was right. He couldn't make her marry him. And, damn it, he wished he could.

"You can't keep me from my child," he warned her.

"I won't even try. I'm betting I won't have to."

"What's that supposed to mean?"

"Ford," she said, shaking her head. "You go through life keeping everyone at arm's length. You don't let anyone close to you. And you're so charming most people don't even notice."

"But you did," he muttered.

"Well, I consider myself something of an expert at holding people at an emotional distance." She flashed him a smile. If he didn't know her so well, he might not have seen the sadness in her gaze. "So I recognized the signs. You have a mother, a step-mom, or whatever she is, and three sisters. Sure, you support them financially. You fix problems for them, but that's the extent of your relationship with them. You don't let them choose. If they're too much of an emotional burden for you, then I'm guessing a baby is way more than you're ready for."

He wanted to argue with her, but the best he could come up with was a grumbled "This isn't over yet."

What could he really say? He *didn't* let anyone close to him. Not even his family. What kind of husband would he make? What kind of father?

Kitty and the baby would be better off without him. The best thing he could do for them was show himself out.

She'd always considered her active social life a part of her job. She didn't have much formal training and had not even graduated college. She wasn't the kind of woman who could inspire the confidence of the board or the stockholders. But there was one area of business in which she excelled. Schmoozing.

For that reason, dinner parties and gala balls

weren't mere social engagements. They were work. Tonight's gallery opening was no different, with one exception. Normally, when she worked a room, it was with the intent of making contacts and keeping her ear to the ground for useful information. But today she wasn't looking for information. She was looking for a spouse.

She may have scoffed at Ford's proposal of marriage, but she had to agree he had a point. Being a single mom would be tough.

But she certainly couldn't marry Ford. She was far too emotionally involved with him. Oh, who was she kidding? She was in love with him. He made her feel things no other man had ever made her feel. But for now, she was hoping that was a temporary condition.

Surely all she needed was some time away from him. Time for her feelings to fade and her heart to heal. And that would never happen if she married him.

And if he asked her again, she might not have the strength to say no.

Her only hope was to go back to her original plan. Find a husband who could help her run Biedermann's. Once she was safely engaged, Ford would leave her alone and she could start the long, arduous process of getting over him. What she needed now was a husband who would care about her baby, but never press her for a truly intimate relationship. Luckily she knew Simon Durant would be the perfect man for the job.

She moved through the crowd, her gaze shifting as she looked for a head of artfully tousled black hair.

Finally, she saw him at the back of the room, his arm draped over the shoulder of a whippet-lean man a good decade younger than he was.

Simon's face brightened when he saw her. "Kitty, darling! With all that nonsense in the news, I didn't think you'd make it."

Simon greeted her with double air kisses to her cheeks. Cosmo, the pretentious young artist whose show this was and whose shoulder Simon had recently been draped over, merely nodded before turning his attention elsewhere. But then, Cosmo had never liked her.

Kitty squeezed Simon's hand in greeting. She nodded in Cosmo's direction as she asked, "Do you think he'll notice if I steal you away for a few minutes?"

"He's talking to an art critic, so I doubt it."

Simon linked his arm with hers and guided her toward the open bar.

"So you've been following the stories in the news?" she asked.

"Mostly no, but the gossip has been hard to avoid. I don't suppose the delicious Mr. Langley is…"

He let his voice trail off suggestively.

"Gay?" she supplied. "Unfortunately, no." But wouldn't this all be much easier if he were? She certainly never would have found herself in her current situation. "I have a problem, Simon, and I think you might be able to help me with it."

They'd reached the bar. Kitty ordered a bottled water and Simon ordered a mango mojito. "You know I'll do anything for you."

She waited until they'd received their drinks and were out of the range of nosy ears before leaning close and saying, "Okay. Then marry me."

Simon choked on his drink, spewing a froth of orange liquid a good three feet. "Marry you? Honey, you're not exactly my type. And I didn't think I was that subtle or you were that dumb."

She smiled. "I'm not. And, for the record, neither are you."

"In that case, why would we get married?"

She sipped her water. "Simon, you're a brilliant businessman, but your family doesn't appreciate you." The Durants owned a chain of hotels. It was a business that had been around almost as long as Biedermann's. However, the Durant family tree was massive, sprawling and loaded with acorns of brilliant businessmen. Unlike her own family tree, which had been winnowed down to her one scrawny branch.

"You're not reaching your full potential at Durant International. You're too far down in the line of succession. Right now you're stuck as—what is it?— junior VP of public relations?"

Simon cringed.

"We both know you're capable of so much more." Kitty leaned forward, her zeal showing just a little as she sensed his interest being piqued. "Marry me, take over as CEO of Biedermann's and we'll kill numerous birds with one stone. You'll get a job you can be proud of and you'll come into your inheritance."

He quirked an eyebrow. "My inheritance, eh?"

"Rumor has it your very conservative grandmother is withholding your inheritance until you marry and settle down."

Simon's eyebrows both shot up. "The rumor mill has been active indeed."

"Is it true, then?"

"Let's just say Grandmother Durant has never approved of my lifestyle, but I have plenty of other sources of income. And I don't care about the money."

"Ah, but you do care about her. And I suspect it bothers you that you've never lived up to her standards. She'd be very pleased if we married. You could even provide her with a great-grandchild."

Emotion flickered across Simon's face, barely visible in the dim lighting of that gallery. Something dark and a little sad. She knew in that instant that her instincts about Simon had been right.

While he was decidedly gay, he regretted some of the things his lifestyle had cost him: his family's respect and the chance for a family of his own. She might just be able to tempt him onto an easier path. They'd never have a real marriage, but they were friends at least. Which was more than some couples could say.

Simon frowned as if he were seriously considering her offer. Hope surged through her. Maybe this would actually work. If it did, it would all be so simple. Such a fine solution to all of her problems.

"And what would you get out of this marriage?" he asked.

"I'd get a talented CEO. With you at the helm, Biedermann's stock would start to climb again. I'd keep the company out of the hands of FMJ. It's so perfect, I almost wonder why I didn't think of it before."

Simon studied her. "I was wondering that myself. After all, you haven't gone to lengths to hide the fact that you've been looking for a husband to bail you out."

She nearly laughed. "Don't tell me I've offended you by not propositioning you before now?"

"Not at all. I'm just curious why you're suddenly so desperate." Simon gave her a piercing look. "You know I'd never be the kind of husband you deserve."

She nodded. "Of course I know that. But we're friends. I think it would be very easy for us to settle into a marriage of sorts."

He cocked his head to the side and asked, "If you're serious, why come here? Why not just call? Why ask now? It's not often a man gets tracked down in the middle of his lover's art show and propositioned."

She had to laugh at that. "It seemed like the kind of thing to discuss in person. And I'm in a bit of a hurry."

"You make a very tempting package, my dear, but—"

"But you're not tempted?" she asked with a sigh.

"It's more that I think you'll regret it later. In my experience, when someone propositions you late at night, on impulse, it's because they're running away from someone else."

"I'm not running away from Ford." But the panicked note in her voice alarmed her.

Simon leveled his gaze at her. "Really? Why don't you tell me what happened?"

"Nothing happened," she insisted, determined to leave it at that. However, she kept talking, seemingly unable to stop the flow of words. "That man is impossible. He's insulting and rude. And he…" She struggled to regain the composure she felt slipping. "And he asked me to marry him."

Before she knew it, she'd told Simon the entire story. From the unplanned pregnancy to her incompetence as a CEO to Ford's offer of marriage.

When she finished, she looked at Simon, fully expecting a flood of sympathy. Instead he gazed at her in that penetrating way of his.

"What?" she asked.

"I'm just trying to figure out why you need me to be your husband and your CEO, if Ford has already offered to do the job."

"I can't accept his proposal. He only offered because he feels sorry for me."

"Sorry for you?" Simon asked.

She fumed. "I think he sees it as a point of honor."

Simon laughed at her. "Sure there's pity sex. But there's no such thing as a pity marriage. No man is that honorable."

Humiliation burned her cheeks as she asked, "Then why would he offer to marry me?"

Simon shrugged. "You'll have to ask him. Maybe he offered for the reason most men ask a woman to marry them. Maybe he loves you."

Shock coursed through her body. Love? Ford might love her? For one awful moment, her heart leaped into her throat, then sanity returned. "That's impossible."

"Are you sure?" Before she could answer, he pressed on. "Do you love him?"

"I don't—" But she could only shake her head. Not in denial, but in confusion. Was what she felt really love? Not a temporary blip of imaginary love, but real love. The kind strong enough to sustain an actual marriage? "I don't know."

"Then you better figure it out." Simon pulled her close and leaned down to brush a kiss across her cheek. But before his lips made contact with her skin, someone yanked him away from her and punched him soundly in the face.

"You didn't have to punch him."

Kitty sat beside Ford in the back of a taxi, but she'd crammed herself as far against the door as she could. Her arms were crossed over her chest as she gazed belligerently forward, her legs crossed away from him so that as she tapped her foot in irritation it scraped against the door. The cab driver kept glaring at her in the mirror, but she ignored him. Occasionally, the driver sent him a pleading look for backup, but Ford ignored him, too. Hell, he had bigger problems. Much, much bigger.

"What were you thinking?" she demanded.

What was he supposed to say to that? He hadn't been thinking. When he'd walked into that gallery and seen another man leaning down to kiss Kitty, he'd simply lost it. Never mind that the man doing the kissing was gay. Ford hadn't known that until after he'd punched him, when a pint-size, flamboyant man had shrieked and run across the room to kneel beside the fallen man. A lot of drama had ensued. Ford figured he was lucky the police hadn't been called, because an arrest was the last thing he needed to add to his humiliation.

To make matters worse, he'd obviously been set up. He'd gone to that art gallery in the first place because half an hour earlier he'd gotten a picture e-mailed to him of Kitty snuggling up to that guy. He'd been furious. It hadn't mattered that the e-mail had been from someone claiming to be Suzy Snark. He'd deal with that issue later. For now, he had more pressing issues.

Kitty shifted in her seat so she was almost facing him. "Do you have anything to say for yourself?" she asked in slow, baffled tones. "Any explanation for why you'd do that?"

There was a note of expectancy in her voice. Was there some answer she wanted him to give? Did she understand his actions? Because he sure as hell didn't.

He glanced at her only briefly before looking back out his window. He didn't know what to say. Because the truth was, he *did* have to hit him. When he'd seen Simon kissing Kitty, the need to hit him had been so strong it had almost been a compulsion.

In that moment, all the heightened emotions of that past week—all the anxiety, all the desire, all the frustration—all that emotion had crystallized into pure, blinding fury.

"Do you have anything to say for yourself? Anything at all?"

"I don't want to talk about it."

She threw up her hands in a *what the hell?* gesture. She snorted, turning toward him. "Of all the stupid—"

"I know. Shut up." He turned to face her, too. "You think I don't know what I did was stupid? I know. I'm thirty-two years old—damn it—I know better than to punch a guy just because he's kissing my woman. I. Know. Better."

Her eyes widened slightly at his words. She looked as if she wanted to turn and run, but in the tight confines of the taxi, there was nowhere to go. And since she wasn't saying anything, he kept talking.

"I'm not a complete moron, despite all evidence to the contrary. I don't fight. That's just not who I am. Back when we were kids, Jonathan got into plenty of fights. Matt, too. But not me. I was always the one talking the other guy into backing down. I've always been too smart to fight." He scrubbed a hand through his hair. "I guess you just bring out the idiot in me."

Her gaze narrowed slightly. "That's all you have to say for yourself?"

"What else do you want me to say?"

"Nothing. Nothing at all." Then she leaned forward and tapped on the glass separating them from the cab driver. "Pull over here," she ordered.

"Come on, Kitty, you can't get out here. It's late and you're a twenty-minute cab ride from your apartment."

"I'm not getting out. You are."

Eleven

Kitty watched Ford climb from the cab with a sinking stomach. If she didn't know it was too early for her to feel the baby moving, she'd have sworn the little bugger was giving her a swift kick in the gut. And not in a good way.

She'd given Ford the perfect opportunity to tell her he loved her. And all he'd come up with was "You just bring out the idiot in me."

That was the best he could do? Not "I love you." Not even "I couldn't stand the sight of another man touching you." Geesh, she would have settled for "I was jealous." But oh, no. That's not what she got. She got "You just bring out the idiot in me."

Well. What could she have said to that? "Gosh, I'm so glad I could help"?

Simon had been wrong.

Ford didn't love her.

But she did love him.

Something she hadn't known for sure until she'd been sitting there beside him in the cab, heart thudding away in her chest, waiting to hear his answer. Praying for a declaration from him.

And the instant he'd made that stupid idiot comment she'd known that she'd been kidding herself until now. She wasn't immune to Ford. He had the power to crush her very soul.

How could she even see him again? How could she risk falling even more in love with him?

No, she needed some distance. Not to mention some time. She had never backed down from a fight in her life, but she knew Ford. He wouldn't leave her alone. He'd never give her heart time to build up calluses. Which meant she had to go into hiding.

A few minutes later when the cab pulled to stop in front of her building, she leaned in the window as she paid. "Can you wait? I'll be down in just a few minutes."

It didn't take her long to pack a bag and return to the waiting cab. It was risky, leaving just now, when the deal with FMJ was still up in the air, but she just couldn't stay. She'd always thought losing Biedermann's was the hardest thing she'd ever have to go through. Turned out she was wrong. Losing Ford was so much harder.

By morning, Ford was ready for some answers. And, frankly, he figured he had them coming. Unfortunately, Kitty was nowhere to be found. She wasn't at work, she wasn't at home. She wasn't even at any of the spas he could think of calling.

In the end, he decided to check with the one person he least wanted to see. Simon Durant.

He tracked Simon down at the other man's apartment on the Upper West Side.

When Simon opened his front door sporting an already bruising black eye, Ford didn't waste any time. He figured the man was seconds away from throwing him out already.

He tried to contain his anger, but it crept into his voice as he asked, "What the hell did you say to Kitty?"

Simon's eyebrows shot up as he gestured for Ford to follow him into the living room. "Why do you assume I said anything to her?"

"Because she's gone."

"Gone?" Simon dropped onto the sofa, stretching out his legs along the seat.

"Yes, gone. As in, she's not answering her phone, she's not at home, and no one can tell me where she is."

"Ahh. I see." Simon nodded sagely, but didn't offer anything else. Then he looked meaningfully at the chair across from him.

Ford sat begrudgingly. This wasn't a social visit, but Simon clearly enjoyed toying with him. "So what did you say to her?"

"Hmm, let me think." Simon tapped his forefinger on his upper lip as if deep in thought. "First she asked me if I would marry her."

Ford had to repress the urge to leap across the coffee table and wrap his hands around the other man's throat. But hitting Simon last night obviously hadn't helped anything, so Ford sat, drumming his fingers on his knees, and prayed that Simon would reach the end of the story before he reached the end of his patience.

"And what did you say?" Ford gave Simon a verbal nudge.

"Well, no. Obviously." Simon sent him a look that seemed to ask, *Are you always this dumb?*

"Obviously."

"And then she told me that you had asked her to marry you. It's all very *Midsummer Night's Dream,* don't you think?"

Ford ignored him and asked, "Then what happened?"

"Then she cried a little." Simon's flippant tone vanished under the weight of this accusation. "And you know, Kitty never cries."

Ford could only swallow and nod.

"Do you know she's under the impression you asked her to marry you because you pity her?"

"That's absurd," Ford said automatically.

"I'm glad you think so." Simon flashed him a wane smile. "That's what I said. I told her I thought you were in love with her."

Ford felt like his stomach dropped out of his body as his mind went wheeling.

"Well?" Simon asked after a minute.

"Well, what?"

"Are you? In love with Kitty, I mean."

"No" was his automatic response, but even as he said the word he felt a pang deep in his heart.

Kitty was probably the most amazing woman he'd ever known. Smart, sexy as hell, and so damn pretty it almost hurt to look at her. None of which was even half as impressive as her pure strength of will. Her independence. In her lifetime, she'd managed to overcome challenges he couldn't even imagine. And she was so damn determined to do it all on her own.

It was kind of ironic. For the first time in his life, he wanted to help someone. He wanted to shoulder all the burdens or to stand by her side when she shouldered them herself. He wanted to be there for her no matter what. Not just for her, but for the baby, too. He wanted to try his hand at being the kind of father he'd never had.

If only she'd let him. Of course he was in love with her. Who wouldn't be? "Yes," he said finally.

This time, the smile Simon sent him was beaming. "Well, then." He straightened. "We have some work to do, don't we?"

If Kitty had any illusions that Ford would come rushing after her to sweep her off her feet, they faded quickly. As one week passed into the next, she faced the possibility that he wasn't coming for her. True, she'd made herself difficult to find, but not impossible. After all, the hotel was just a few blocks down from Biedermann's headquarters.

At first, she mostly just sulked. It wasn't so much that

she expected him to find her, but rather that she hoped he would. In her mind she replayed scenes from all the classic romantic movies she'd watched growing up. The ones where the man chases down the heroine on New Year's Eve or at the Empire State Building to declare his eternal love. She wanted their story to have that kind of ending, even though she knew it was impossible.

When she wasn't entertaining romantic fantasies about Ford, she ate and slept, the two activities her doctor most approved of. She was surprised how tired being pregnant made her feel, but thankful that lots of rest and near constant eating kept the nausea at bay.

As far as work was concerned, she turned over the negotiations with FMJ to Marty. Following Ford's advice, she came clean to Marty about her dyslexia. He was shocked, but far more sympathetic than she'd imagined he'd be. He called daily with updates about the acquisition, but she found it hard to care.

Still, she knew the negotiations had not yet been finalized. So when Casey came by for a visit and mentioned that Ford had scheduled another press conference, she was immediately suspicious. If Ford was ready to talk to the press, it could mean only one thing. If he wasn't going to announce that the deal was finalized, did that mean FMJ was pulling out?

Whether she was ready to face him or not, it was time for her to come out of hiding.

Staring out at the sea of reporters, Ford had to swallow down his nerves. He'd done dozens of these things in the past, hell, maybe hundreds, and they'd never bothered him at all.

But he knew if he had any chance of winning Kitty back, it would be right now. And she was out there somewhere, just waiting to see what he had up his sleeve.

He'd known—of course—that the one sure way to guarantee she came to the press conference was to tell Casey to keep her away.

He didn't have long to worry about it, because before he knew it, Matt was giving him the nod that it was time to begin.

"Acquiring Biedermann Jewelry was quite the departure for FMJ. Up until now, we've been known for pioneering green technologies. However, we were confident that with the right leadership and creativity Biedermann's could once again become a leader in the industry.

"Though our agreement with Biedermann's hasn't been finalized, we're so enthusiastic about the new direction we're taking things we wanted to give everyone a sneak peek at what we're doing.

"Casey there is passing out swag bags, and if you'll look inside, you'll see what I'm talking about. We're launching a line of stylish accessories for personal mobile devices."

A murmur went through the crowd as people began digging through the bags. Each of the twenty bags contained the Victorian-inspired iPhone case and the gothic Bluetooth earpiece. The earpiece had taken the most work, but luckily Matt had figured out a way to retrofit an earpiece FMJ was already manufacturing.

"These are all just beta versions," Ford continued over the whispers. He smiled broadly. "So go easy on them. The final versions will be in stores within a few months, along with the rest of the line. All of which, by the way, are designed personally by Kitty Biedermann herself."

Kitty could not have been more surprised than anyone else in the audience. She sat in the back row, feeling a little like Jackie O. hidden under sunglasses and a hat. So far, no one had recognized her.

When she'd opened the bag Casey had handed her with a wink, she'd actually gasped aloud. Thankfully her gasp was one of many exclamatory noises, so she didn't think anyone had noticed.

She dumped the two boxes on her lap and then carefully opened the first, unwrapping the tissue paper that surrounded the iPhone case. Her hand trembled as she held it. It was something she'd never dreamed she'd see. Her design come to life, strange and a little absurd though it was, with its Victorian curlicues and its gothic clawed feet.

After a lifetime of dreaming of it, she was finally holding one of her creations in her hands. Even better, the people on either side of her were murmuring excitedly. Her father had been wrong. There was a market for her work.

And Ford had given it to her.

By the time she returned her attention to the press conference, Ford was answering questions.

"Will Ms. Biedermann continue to design the line?" one reporter asked.

"I certainly hope so. As you can see, her designs are very original."

"Does this mean she won't be serving as CEO of Biedermann's?"

"Ms. Biedermann is extremely smart and talented. Like many other people who are dyslexic, she's shown tremendous resilience in overcoming her disability. Needless to say, FMJ will be happy to have her in whatever capacity she chooses to fill."

Kitty's head snapped up as panic poured through her body. He'd just casually dropped her dyslexia into the conference like it was nothing. What was he *doing?*

Ford had paused as shock rippled through the crowd, but now he continued. "Her learning disability has made her job as CEO extremely difficult, as you can imagine."

"So then she won't be continuing on in her current position? FMJ is going to replace her?" one of the reporters asked.

Ford's gaze sought out Kitty where she sat in the back of the room. He'd seen her trying to blend in when she'd first arrived. Not that Kitty could disappear in a crowd. Her intrinsic style and grace made her stand out.

When he'd made the announcement about her dyslexia, she'd near leaped to her feet. She yanked off her sunglasses and was glaring at him through the crowd. Was she anxious to hear his answer or sending him a telepathic message to explode? He couldn't tell. For now, all he could do was answer the reporter's question as honestly as he could.

"On the contrary. FMJ is going to do everything in its power to support her in whatever she decides. Biedermann's is still her company. However, the position she holds within the company will ultimately be her decision."

After that, he answered a few more questions and then wrapped up his part. He neatly handed the podium over to Matt to talk about the specs just as they'd planned. He wanted to slip out quietly. The last thing he wanted now was to get waylaid by some nosy reporter. No, there was only one person he wanted to talk to right now. And only one question he wanted answers to. Now that he'd revealed her biggest secret to the world, would she still want to talk to him?

She caught up with him right outside the conference room, falling into step beside him as if it hadn't been nearly two weeks since he'd seen her. As if there weren't repeated marriage proposals hanging in the air between them.

Finally the tension got to him and he broke the silence. "They seemed enthusiastic about the new line."

She slanted him a look, but the sunglasses were back on and he couldn't read her expression. "It was a big risk announcing it this early."

"It was. But Biedermann's stock price has been

climbing steadily since I scheduled the press conference. It had been fluctuating based on the Suzy Snark blogs. No matter what happens, Biedermann's is no longer in danger of being delisted."

After today, she would be fine even without him, if that's what she chose.

She stopped him, placing a hand on his arm. "Why did you do it? If our stock prices are climbing then theoretically I don't have to accept your buyout offer now. You made it easier for me to walk away from you."

"That's one way to look at it." He grinned wolfishly. "But all of Matt's Bluetooth stuff is proprietary technology. If you want Biedermann's to actually sell those gadgets of yours, now you have to sign the papers."

"So it was a trap?"

They'd reached the hotel lobby by now, and she stopped cold. He turned to face her. He'd been wondering when they would get to this part of the discussion. The part where she ripped him a new one for spilling the beans about her dyslexia.

But instead of the blazing anger he expected to read in her expression, he saw only shattering vulnerability.

"You can't honestly expect me to trust you after this. After you—" Her voice broke. Without meeting his gaze she pushed past him to walk briskly through the hotel lobby.

He caught up with her in a few steps. Grabbing her arm, he turned her to face him. "I brought up your dyslexia in the press conference to prove you can trust me."

"That makes perfect sense. Betray someone's trust to prove that they can trust you." She tugged on her arm, glaring at him. "Except I hadn't even trusted you enough to tell you about my dyslexia. You wheedled that information out of my assistant."

She used the word *wheedled* with relish. Obviously she remembered he'd objected to it the last time.

"No, you're right," he told her. "You didn't tell me. But then you didn't tell Casey, either. I can almost excuse you not trusting me. But Casey? That kid would do anything for you." He shook his head in exasperation. "Have you ever wondered what all this deception has cost you?"

She stared at him blankly, as if she didn't understand his words, but at least she was listening.

He tipped her chin up so she was looking full at him. For a second he studied her face, taking in the lines of strain around her mouth, the clear green intensity of her eyes. Her perfectly kissable bow of a mouth, painted a tempting scarlet.

His heart seized in his chest. He may have royally screwed this up. If she didn't forgive him, this may be the last time he was this close to her. But he couldn't think about that now.

"Kitty, your family made you believe your dyslexia was something to hide. Something to be ashamed of. But it's not. It's—"

"Don't try to tell me it's no big deal. That it doesn't make me different than anyone else." She twisted her chin away. "Because it is a big deal. It makes everything harder."

"Which is exactly why you need to be able to ask for help. You need to surround yourself with people you trust." His frustration crept into his voice. "No one does everything on their own. The rest of us mere mortals need help all the time. Why shouldn't you?"

But she just shook her head. "You don't get it, do you? This was my secret. It wasn't yours to tell."

"Exactly. And you were never going to tell it. You would have let people go on thinking the worst of you forever rather than have even one moment of vulnerability. So I made the decision for you. I did it because it was the right thing for you.

"For once in my life, I did the right thing, not just the easy thing." He laughed wryly. "I could have just left things as they were. I probably could have even talked my way back into your bed." He waited for her to protest, but she didn't. They both knew he was right on that account. "Instead, I did that one thing that I knew would piss you off, because I knew it would make your life better."

"So you did it because you wanted to piss me off?"

"No. I did it because I love you."

Kitty's heart, which had been racing with fury and fear, seemed to stop in her chest. She squeezed her eyes shut for a second as emotion flooded her.

He *loved* her?

When she opened her eyes he was still there. Watching her expectantly. "Look, neither of us is any good at this. We're both slow to trust. Neither of us let other people close. And it would undoubtedly be easier on both of us if we walked away right now. But I don't want to do that, and I'm betting you don't want to do that, either."

She opened her mouth to speak, but her throat closed off and all she could do was shake her head mutely.

"So I say we decide right now. We stick with this and make it work."

She wanted to believe him, but her heart didn't know how to trust what her mind heard.

"Biedermann's—" she began.

His hand tightened around her arm. "This doesn't have anything to do with Biedermann's. This is about you and me. And the baby we're going to have." He paused, his gaze dropping from her eyes to her belly. "I love you, Kitty. And I want to be a father to our baby. The only question is, do you trust me enough to let me?"

Her heart stuttered in her chest. Did she trust him? The question had barely flitted through her mind before she knew the answer. Of course she did.

An unexpected bubble of laughter rose up in her throat. Ford cocked an eyebrow at her giggle, his expression still expectant. But before he could ask why she was laughing, she threw her arms around his neck.

"Of course I trust you. Which is so silly because just a few minutes ago I didn't think I did."

She felt his arms wrap around her and tighten, felt his face nuzzle into her hair. Only when she felt the shudder of his deep breath did she realize how nervous he must have been.

She pulled back to meet his gaze. "You know I love you, too, right?"

His lips quirked into a half smile. "I thought my chances were pretty good."

"What would you have done if I'd have said no?"

"I'm not the kind of guy who takes no for an answer."

"Meaning?" she asked.

"Meaning, I would have pursued you until you said yes."

Just a few weeks ago, that answer would have infuriated her. Now she knew it was just exactly what she needed. *He* was just exactly what she needed.

She forced a mock frown. "You know, that was pretty gutsy. Asking a jewelry heiress to marry you when you didn't even have a ring to offer."

To her surprise he smiled broadly. "Hey, this I have covered." He reached into his pocket, pulled out something small. When he opened his palm, he revealed a single earring shaped like a bird.

"My earring," she gasped. She picked up the earring and let it dangle between her fingers. "I thought it was lost forever. I can't believe you kept it all this time."

He cupped her cheek in his palm. "Maybe I was just waiting for the right time to give it back to you."

As he pulled her into his arms one more time, she thought back to the first night they'd met. Maybe part of her knew even then that he was the perfect man for her. Or maybe she was just very, very lucky.

Either way, she was smart enough to hold on tight to this wonderful man and never let him go.

Epilogue

From the blog of New York gossip columnist Suzy Snark:

Faithful readers of this column have no doubt been disappointed with the lack of drama in Kitty Biedermann's life. Ever since her springtime wedding to hunky business magnate Ford Langley, her life has been dreadfully dull. But that is all about to change. Late last night, with all the theatrics one would expect from Kitty's daughter, Ilsa Marie Biedermann-Langley made her first appearance.

The tiny diva will be living at her family's full-time home in Palo Alto, California, but you can expect frequent visits to the city. After all, Kitty's new line of accessories are the must-have items of the season, once again putting Biedermann Jewelry at the top of the fashion food chain.

"Ilsa made the Suzy Snark column," Ford said, looking up from his laptop.

Kitty's head snapped up. "She did?" Her gaze narrowed. "That Suzy Snark better watch it. If she—"

"Don't worry, it's all good stuff." Still, he chuckled at his wife's fierce reaction. It was their first morning back from the hospital. He and Kitty were sitting quietly at the table, him with his laptop, her with her sketchpad. Baby Ilsa slept quietly in the bassinet they'd rolled into the kitchen. For the moment, all was peaceful and quiet. Not that it would be for long. He could already tell that Ilsa had her mother's sassy temper. Which was just the way he liked it.

* * * * *

*Fan favorite Leslie Kelly is bringing her
readers a fantasy so scandalous,
we're calling it FORBIDDEN!*

Look for
PLAY WITH ME
Available February 2010
from Harlequin® Blaze™.

"Aren't you going to say 'Fly me' or at least 'Welcome Aboard'?"

Amanda Bauer didn't. The softly muttered word that actually came out of her mouth was a lot less welcoming. And had fewer letters. Four, to be exact.

The man shook his head and tsked. "Not exactly the friendly skies. Haven't caught the spirit yet this morning?"

"Make one more airline-slogan crack and you'll be walking to Chicago," she said.

He nodded once, then pushed his sunglasses onto the top of his tousled hair. The move revealed blue eyes that matched the sky above. And yeah. They were twinkling. Damn it.

"Understood. Just, uh, promise me you'll say 'Coffee, tea or me' at least once, okay? Please?"

Amanda tried to glare, but that twinkle sucked the

annoyance right out of her. She could only draw in a slow breath as he climbed into the plane. As she watched her passenger disappear into the small jet, she had to wonder about the trip she was about to take.

Coffee and tea they had, and he was welcome to them. But her? Well, she'd never even considered making a move on a customer before. Talk about unprofessional.

And yet…

Something inside her suddenly wanted to take a chance, to be a little outrageous.

How long since she had done indecent things—or decent ones, for that matter—with a sexy man? Not since before they'd thrown all their energies into expanding Clear-Blue Air, at the very least. She hadn't had time for a lunch date, much less the kind of lust-fest she'd enjoyed in her younger years. The kind that lasted for entire weekends and involved not leaving a bed except to grab the kind of sensuous food that could be smeared onto—and eaten off—someone else's hot, naked, sweat-tinged body.

She closed her eyes, her hand clenching tight on the railing. Her heart fluttered in her chest and she tried to make herself move. But she couldn't—not climbing up, but not backing away, either. Not physically, and not in her head.

Was she really considering this? God, she hadn't even looked at the stranger's left hand to make sure he was available. She had no idea if he was actually attracted to her or just an irrepressible flirt. Yet something inside was telling her to take a shot with this man.

It was crazy. Something she'd never considered. Yet right now, at this moment, she was definitely considering it. If he was available…could she do it? Seduce a stranger. Have an anonymous fling, like something out of a blue movie on late-night cable?

She didn't know. All she knew was that the flight to Chicago was a short one so she had to decide quickly. And as she put her foot on the bottom step and began to climb up, Amanda suddenly had to wonder if she was about to embark on the ride of her life.

Sold, bought, bargained for or bartered

He'll take his…

Bride on Approval

Whether there's a debt to be paid,
a will to be obeyed or a business
to be saved…she has no choice
but to say, "I do"!

PURE PRINCESS,
BARTERED BRIDE

by *Caitlin Crews*

#2894

Available February 2010!

HARLEQUIN® *Blaze*™

*It all started
with a few naughty books....*

As a member of the Red Tote Book Club,
Carol Snow has been studying works of
classic erotic literature...but Carol doesn't
believe in love...or marriage. It's going to take
another kind of classic—Charles Dickens's
A Christmas Carol—and a little otherworldly
persuasion to convince her to go after her
own sexily ever after.

Cuddle up with

Her Sexy Valentine

by STEPHANIE BOND

Available February 2010

HARLEQUIN® HISTORICAL:
Where love is timeless

From chivalrous knights
to roguish rakes, look for the
variety Harlequin® Historical
has to offer every month.

HARLEQUIN
Ambassadors

Want to share your passion for reading Harlequin® Books?

Become a Harlequin Ambassador!

Harlequin Ambassadors are a group
of passionate and well-connected readers
who are willing to share their joy of reading
Harlequin® books with family and friends.

You'll be sent all the tools you need to spark
great conversation, including free books!

All we ask is that you share the romance
with your friends and family!

You'll also be invited to have a say in
new book ideas and exchange opinions
with women just like you!

To see if you qualify* to be a Harlequin Ambassador, please visit
www.HarlequinAmbassadors.com.

*Please note that not everyone who applies to be a Harlequin Ambassador will
qualify. For more information please visit www.HarlequinAmbassadors.com.

Thank you for your participation.

BAP09BPA

REQUEST YOUR FREE BOOKS!

2 FREE NOVELS PLUS 2 FREE GIFTS!

Passionate, Powerful, Provocative!

SDES10